A Knight With Mercy

An Assassin Knights novel

Book 2

by

Laurel O'Donnell

Dearest Reader –

Thank you for reading A Knight with Mercy! I'm glad you picked up my novel.

I want to warn you, this novel contains content that may be controversial and difficult for some readers. My goal in writing this story was not to offend anyone nor demean any victims or survivors, but to tell a tale of love overcoming evil.

I hope you enjoy Richard and Mercy's tale. Prepare yourself! Let me take you into a different time. A different place!

Welcome to my world!

Laurel

Chapter One

1172
Goodmont, England

"**For** the love of my lord William!"

The words echoed throughout the black darkness. Richard le Breton gripped his sword tightly, knowing what was to come. He wanted to drop the weapon and back away, but his fingers would not open. Suddenly, as he tried to force his fingers open, blood pooled from between them to drip down his arms into the blackness. A balding man with white hair on the sides of his head and an immaculate white robe towered up to an unreasonable monstrous height.

Richard tossed in his bed, kicking at his covers. He knew that man. The Archbishop of Canterbury, Thomas Becket.

As Richard watched, horrified, and unable to stop it, the top the of the Archbishop's pristine head split open as if from the blow of an axe, the wound growing wider and wider. Blood was everywhere, turning the black around him into red guilt. Richard tried to pull back, but his feet were stuck in the red liquid; the blood-like tar sucking at his booted feet.

Around Richard, flames erupted, the heat singing the flesh from his arms. He pulled back, but the fire was everywhere. He looked up at the Archbishop in desperation.

With half of his head gone, the Archbishop pointed a finger at Richard. "You did this."

Richard sat up, his body slick with sweat. He turned his head, gazing this way and that. When his rapid breathing slowed, he wiped at his brow and inspected the sleeve of his tunic in the moonlight, fearful that he would find blood. But there was no marking on his sleeve. Just his body's reaction to the dream; a dream he often had. He swung his legs from the straw mattress, and the blanket entwined around his legs fell to the wooden floor. He rested his head in his hands, taking a deep breath to calm his madly beating heart before running his hands through his hair, and rising. There would be no further sleep this night.

He rose, pulled on his boots and secured his belt to his waist. He moved to the door, threw it open and emerged into the hallway. He looked down the stairway at the first floor of the inn where the flickering glow of a warm fire danced on the walls. He walked down the stairs and stood at the bottom, scanning the room. The hearth light washed over empty tables and chairs scattered throughout. When he saw the room was vacant, he let out a long breath and took a seat before the fire. He extended his hands toward the hearth, feeling the warmth against his palms. He couldn't forget it. The murder weighed heavy on his shoulders even though it happened eighteen months ago. There was no escaping the guilt that followed him like a shadow.

A young girl walked up to him. Richard recognized her as the innkeeper's daughter. He had seen the innkeeper giving the girl orders when he had arrived. The child rubbed her eyes as if she had just woken. "Is there somethin' I can get ya?"

"No, lass," Richard said.

The girl nodded and turned away, disappearing into a darkened back room.

Richard stared into the snapping flames of the hearth, running a hand absently over his long beard. After the death of Becket, King Henry had advised all four of the knights involved to flee England. Richard shook his head. England. His home. They had killed the Archbishop under King Henry's orders, and he had advised them to run away. He sighed. He couldn't blame Henry. The King couldn't risk being excommunicated and losing favor with his people. At least he had not stripped them of their titles and lands. His friend and co-conspirator, Sir Hugh de Morville, had lands and a castle at Knaresborough where the four knights had lived since the death of Becket. When the Pope excommunicated them in March of 1171, they had done everything to gain an audience with him to beg forgiveness. When they had finally faced him and told him of their remorse, it had done no good. He hadn't believed they were truly repentant. He had exiled them to Jerusalem for fourteen years.

Fourteen years. Richard's shoulders sagged. He was on his way to the coast to seek passage to Jerusalem now. He wished he could do it all over again. He would never have harmed the Archbishop. But he could not take it back.

The door swung open and a group of men, farmers by the looks of their dirty tunics and breeches, entered. One nodded toward him. "There he is."

Tingles raced along Richard's spine.

"Is it him?" another asked.

Richard stood. He faced the men as they entered the room. "I want no trouble, friends."

One of the farmers spit on the floor. "We're no friends

of yers, ya murderin' giglet."

Richard turned toward the stairway as one of the farmers rushed to block his path.

"It's him," the innkeeper said to the farmers.

"Ya killed the Archbishop."

Prickles raced across the nape of his neck. How could he deny their accusations? He had been hiding from the fact for years.

When he didn't deny it, the crowd of men murmured unhappily. Dangerously. "It *is* you! Blackguard!"

"Ya'll burn in hell!"

His body jerked forward as someone shoved him from behind. He stumbled forward but caught himself on a chair before he could go down to his hands and knees. More unhappy grumbling sounded in the room as he straightened. He turned to face them, and a solid blow to his chin spun his head back.

"Devil spawn!"

Pain pulsated from his jaw, and he put up his hands up in submission. When one man with dark hair and crooked teeth came toward him, he brought his hand back for a blow. Suddenly, he froze, staring into the farmer's dark hateful eyes. These were innocent men. He had sworn to protect the innocent. It was part of his oath as a knight. He had made that mistake once. He would not do it again. His hesitation was enough. The hateful eyed man raised his fist and swung landing powerfully against Richard's jaw. Another blow to his head knocked him sideways, and the room swirled. Bright flashing lights blinded him for a moment.

Angry grumbling sounded in his ears.

When the blinking lights cleared, his gaze found the door over their shoulders. He had to get out. But there were so many of them in the way.

They closed around him and he lifted his arms to protect himself, to block the blows, but they came quickly, one after the other. They landed with dull thumps followed by body aches. When he turned to defend himself, another blow would land on his unprotected side. There were too many. He heard a hiss and wasn't sure if it was from one of the men or the fire in the hearth. Another painful blow and he clenched his teeth with agony. Was this what he was praying for all these years? To be put out of his misery? Was this his redemption?

A blow to his stomach doubled him over as a hot fire of pain spread from his mid-section through his body.

Was this his end?

He was shoved and then hit hard across his head. The room whirled, spinning as if he were tied to a wheel. Richard was pushed again, and he fell forward to his knee, scraping it on the wooden floor. Was this what the Archbishop endured? His head pounded and his mind returned to the cathedral and the image of Becket on his knees. The thought sent mental agony through him, only enhancing his resolve not to fight back. A punch to his cheek and he tasted copper. Blood.

"Get him!"

The blows fell about him like rain, each landing a stinging agony. He was knocked to the ground, instinctively curling into a ball to protect himself. The kicks began then. Something struck him in his side, knocking the breath from him. He heard men's voices.

"Evil cumberworld!"

"Murderin' arse!"

He pulled his arms around his head, uselessly trying to protect himself and secretly wishing they would use a sword to speed it along.

"Stop!" A voice rang out above the clamor of the others. "Stop!"

He lowered his arms from his head, cautiously, angry that someone should stop his punishment. His death.

Faces hovered over him, twisted with smirks of hate.

One even landed another blow to his head before he could cover it again.

"Stop!"

He looked out between his arms again. Through a haze of pain and blackness eating away at the edges of his vision, he saw an angel emerge from the throng of hatred and contempt. She had soft skin and a concerned look in her blue eyes. Brown hair tumbled in waves over her shoulders as she bent to him.

Behind her, the men grumbled their protest. "He deserves worse!"

The words rang in his head as the darkness consumed his vision.

"No," she said, and knelt at his side. "He is our salvation."

Chapter Two

Mercy Brooker looked down at the wounded knight. Walter, her good friend and nearby neighbor, had helped her move him here, to her barn, where she tended his injuries as best she could while he was unconscious. Cushioned on a bed of straw and covered with a blanket, he was as comfortable as she could make him. His face, framed by brown, wavy hair, was barely recognizable. Discoloration had set in around his left eye and the opposite cheek. His lower lip was cut and puffy. She had removed his tunic to check for further wounds but had found none. She had checked for broken bones, but there were none. She had done all she could for him and yet, he had not regained consciousness. Blows to the head were the most dangerous. She had seen many die from such injuries. And she needed him to live.

"He doesn't look like he's in any shape to be anyone's salvation."

Mercy scowled at the woman standing beside her. Abbey Webb, one of the villages finest weavers, was her closest friend, more like a sister to her. "He'll be fine," Mercy reassured her, but she wasn't certain he would be.

"When he recovers, he'll be a strong knight ready to defend us."

"He killed the Archbishop. Do you think we should put our faith in him?"

"We have no one else." Mercy picked up the bloody cloth and the water basin and turned with Abbey to return to the cottage. She stopped in the doorway to look back at him. A beam of moonlight shone in through a gap in the side wall. The muted light fell over his face. The color around his eye was darkening. His lip was extended and swollen. But there was something about him. Something strong and strangely hypnotic. Maybe it was because she was putting all her hope in him. Maybe because he had come in answer to her prayer.

She chuckled softly, self-mockingly. She was desperate. It was foolish to put all her hope in one man, one man who might not survive the night.

Abbey reached for the door to exit, but Mercy caught her hand. "Don't worry, Abbey. We'll find a way to save Luke."

"You have to give him to the bishop," Abbey whispered. "He *could* be our salvation."

"That's not the answer, Abbey."

Abbey yanked her hand from Mercy's hold. "It is! Maybe the bishop won't take Luke then. Maybe…"

Mercy shook her head. "Do you really believe that?"

Abbey looked down. "I have to. He's coming for Luke in three days. I have to believe we can stop him." She shook her head. "What else can we do?"

Mercy stared at her friend. "Stick to the plan. Can you do that?"

Abbey looked doubtful. "Then what is the knight for?"

"To defend us, if we need him. To fight for us."

"He's unconscious! He's in no shape to fight."

Mercy looked back toward him. "He'll get better."

"But if we give him to the bishop –"

"Abbey, the bishop will take the knight and then take Luke, and all of our hope will be gone."

Abbey sighed and her shoulders sagged. "I can't lose Luke. I don't know what I would do."

Mercy wrapped her arms around her friend, holding her tightly. "I'll be right there with you."

Abbey nodded but worry creased the lines in her forehead.

Mercy followed her out of the barn, closing the door softly behind her.

Walter, her friend and neighbor, greeted them outside. He had a hand on his back, rubbing it gently. He swiped a strand of his gray hair from his forehead and straightened when they emerged. "We should have left him at the inn." He took the basin of water from her hands.

She looked at Walter. She patted his arm with affection. "You did fine."

"I'm sorry. Truly, I am. If I had my way, I would have left him in the woods to die." He ran a hand through his grey hair as he tucked the basin beneath one arm. "You're alone here, Mercy. I don't like leaving him here."

"We'll be fine. You can go. You need to get some sleep before dawn."

Walter scowled. "I'll check back after dinner on the morrow." They walked to the doorway of the cottage. Abbey entered ahead of them.

Mercy thought of her patient. The knight. One of the four knights who had attacked and killed Archbishop Becket. The townsmen had attacked him ruthlessly, even though she doubted they knew which knight he was. It didn't matter. Most of the men thought all of the knights should be dead for attacking the Archbishop. "Do you know which knight he is?"

Walter gave a curt chuckle. "The one that got whooped at the inn." He handed the basin back to her. "You should bind him."

Mercy shook her head. "No. He's too weak. He's no threat to us."

Walter shook his head. "Don't trust him, Mercy. You'd be wise to hand him over to the bishop."

"No," Mercy said stubbornly. He was their last hope. Their *only* hope.

"He's got a one-way pass to Hell. All the knights who killed the Archbishop do. Don't get involved with him."

Unfortunately, Mercy needed his help. She had stopped the men from killing him, he owed her.

"Think of your boy. Think of Kit."

"I *am*. He's who I'm doing this for."

"What will you tell Kit?"

"Nothing. Nothing at all." She looked down at the basin. "He doesn't have to know."

"He'll find out. You can't keep this a secret. The bishop will find out, too."

"I just need time. Time for the knight to recover."

Walter shook his head in disapproval. "A few of the men in the village already know you have him. This is dangerous for you."

"I have to do it, Walter. There is no other choice." Her insides tightened in desperation, in fear. "I only have eight days. And Abbey has less. What else can I do?" Her voice broke. "I won't give Kit up. I won't."

Walter nodded, placing a comforting hand on her shoulder. "Alright. For now, we'll keep him a secret. We'll think of something."

Mercy agreed. "Thank you." But the anxiety and fear were back, simmering inside of her. She would not give up her child.

After Abbey left for her home with her son Luke, Mercy

stayed up. She was hopeful. For the first time in a long time, she had hope. Real hope. She stirred the pot of porridge simmering over the fire in the hearth, waiting for Kit to wake. She tried to think of something to tell the men of the village. Her worst fear was that one of them would tell the bishop. She had no doubt he would punish her for keeping the knight a secret.

A noise startled her out of her reverie, and she turned to find Kit entering the main room, rubbing sleep from his eyes. He was a thin, energetic boy of only four, almost five summers. Five summers. Tremors of unease snaked down her spine.

"Mum?" Kit called.

"Here, Kit," she answered.

"Why are you up already?" he asked, taking a seat at the table.

"Someone needed my help."

"You are always helping someone."

She placed a bowl full of porridge before him. "It's what your father taught me. It's what I know. And it is the right thing to do. I will always help those in need."

"What did they need?"

Mercy looked at Kit. His riotous golden curls stuck up in strange angles from his head. She smoothed them down. "There was a fight."

"Was anyone stabbed?" he asked, licking the side of the bowl.

"Kit! What type of question is that?"

"That's what you do. You stop them from dying when they are hurt." Kit lifted the bowl to his lips.

Mercy stared at her child, his blonde, unruly hair; his small, pudgy fingers. He thought she stopped people from dying. Kit saw her as more than she was. She could not prevent death, only help heal injuries. She had seen death numerous times and been helpless to prevent it. She should correct him. He should know that even his mother couldn't stop people from dying.

He put the bowl on the table and turned to look at her with his large blue eyes.

Her heart melted. He thought she was more than she was. And for a moment, she would let him believe it.

"Aren't you eating?" Kit wondered.

"I already did." She couldn't help bending and pressing a kiss to his curls. "I have to make my rounds. Alice will be here soon. She'll watch you while I make my rounds."

"I don't need to be watched," Kit pouted.

Mercy was glad Walter's wife could help her. She didn't want to leave Kit alone, even if he thought he didn't need Alice.

"Luke went home?"

Mercy nodded, taking a bag of instruments and setting it on the table.

"Are you going to see that magic man?"

"Magic man?" Mercy asked with a scowl of confusion.

"Magi…" Kit mirrored her frown as he concentrated on the word.

And then Mercy understood. He had either overheard her or someone else talking. "Magistrate."

"Yes!"

"No." She began to sort through the instruments in the bag, mentally going over what she needed. "One of the baker's wife's teeth hurts. And the blacksmith hit his thumb on the forge."

"That would hurt!"

"That's why I'm going to see him." She pulled the string tight on the bag to close it and knelt before him. "Kit, I want you to stay out of the barn for a while."

He looked at her with those innocent blue eyes and blinked. "Why?"

For a moment, Mercy thought of concocting a story to keep him out of the barn, but she didn't want to lie to him.

She let out her breath in a slow whoosh. "There is a man recovering from the fight in the barn. I'm not certain if he would harm you or not."

"What about you?"

"Me?"

"Will he harm you?"

She smiled gently. "He had no weapons. Only armor."

Kit gasped. "Is he a knight?"

"He is. But it's important you don't go into the barn. Not until I get to know him."

"Who will protect you?"

She warmed at his concern over her. They were all each had. She patted her waist where she always kept a sheathed dagger. "I always have protection."

Kit huffed in disapproval, crossing his arms over his chest.

"I have a very important job for you." Kit looked at her dubiously and she continued, "His horse is tied behind the barn. Can you feed it and give it water?"

His eyes lit. "Is it a warhorse?"

"No. Palfrey. But it needs someone to take care of it. Can you help me with that duty?"

Kit nodded grudgingly. "I'd rather clean his weapons."

"He had only a dagger."

"Can Luke help with the horse?"

Mercy grinned. "Of course."

"And Joshua?"

Joshua was Kit's imaginary friend. If anyone knew of his friend, they might call it witchcraft. Or worse. She allowed him the fantasy because Joshua had materialized shortly after her husband, his father, had died. "Perhaps you should keep Joshua away from the horse. He might spook it."

Kit nodded in agreement. "Joshua won't like that."

Mercy grasped her son's small hands, drawing his gaze. "Remember to keep Joshua a secret."

Kit nodded, and a strand of blonde hair fell before his intelligent eyes. "I remember."

She kissed his head and moved to the door, pausing. She looked back at her son. He was the world to her. And the future looked so dark for them. She loved him so. "Don't forget about the horse. And remember to be careful. The horse doesn't know you." Kit nodded. "And stay out of the barn."

Mercy picked up the bag from the table. "I'll be home soon."

When Mercy returned from checking on the villagers, it was just after noon. She had been anxious leaving Walter's wife, Alice, with the knight. She had been more anxious leaving her son with instructions not to enter the barn. It was too tempting for a young boy.

When she rode up, Alice, a thin, elderly woman with gray hair tied back into a braid, was pacing before the barn, wringing her wrinkled hands.

Mercy dismounted, fear tightening her stomach. "What is it? Is Kit hurt?"

Alice shook her head, a lock of grey hair falling free from the braid. "A fever. The knight's burning up."

Mercy shoved the reins of her horse into Alice's hands and hurried inside the barn, rushing to the back stall where the knight had been resting. Sunlight shone through a slot of wood on the wall, casting the knight in a subdued light. She dropped to her knees at his side and pressed her hand to his forehead and then his grizzled cheeks. He was overly warm.

"Alice!" she called.

Alice hurried in.

"Get more blankets. Use the ones from my room. Bring a bucket of water and some cloth."

Alice nodded and hurried out of the barn.

Mercy quickly checked his wounds, making sure there was clean cloth covering them for protection. When he began to toss his head and groan, Mercy placed her hand against his cheek, whispering, "It will be alright. Quiet, now."

Suddenly, his eyes snapped open, pinning her to the spot. His hand caught hers, holding it tightly to his cheek. "Hellfire!" he whispered.

Startled, Mercy could only gaze in horror at his utterance.

"Hellfire," he said softly, and seemed to settle back.

Scowling, Mercy eased her hand from his hold and adjusted the blanket over his chest.

He shoved the cloth from his chest and began to toss his head again.

Hellfire? Was he seeing something she couldn't? The uttered word sent chills down her spine. Was he closer to death than she realized? No. She would not let him go without a fight. He was their only hope. *Her* only hope.

Alice entered holding a blanket, and a basin on top of it. Mercy stood and took the basin from her to settle it beside him. She dipped some cloth into the water and wrung it out before placing it across his forehead.

"Maybe we should let him die," Alice stated.

"Alice!"

"Think on it. His death might gain us favor with the bishop."

Mercy snorted. "Nothing can gain us favor with him."

"We could try."

Mercy shook her head as she gazed down at the knight. His dark hair was plastered to his head in sweat. His eye was swollen, as was his lip. So many had wished for his death or suggested turning him over to the bishop. He was alone. "A man that has nothing to lose is worth more than death to us."

Mercy stayed with the knight, dabbing his head and trying to keep him comfortable. He had opened his unswollen eye once or twice in the night and looked at her. She whispered calming words to him. He never spoke of Hellfire again. As she watched him, she thought it might be a good idea if she cut his hair. She had dye in the cottage to disguise his hair. He definitely needed to shave. All of it so others would not recognize him.

Alice stopped in the barn just after dark to inform her Kit was asleep and she would return in the morning. Mercy slept off and on, dreaming of a knight in fire slaying a white dragon.

In the morning, she checked on the knight again, pressing her palm to his forehead and cheeks. The fever had broken. Relief washed over her. He had managed to fight his way through the fever. Now, if he would only open his eyes.

She set about disguising him by cutting his hair in a bowl cut fashion and dying his hair black. It took time and she was careful, washing out the excess in a bucket. It was like painting. She had never dyed anyone's hair before, but she had cut Dean's and Kit's hair numerous times. When she was satisfied with the job, she sat back and gazed at him. He looked different, but she still wanted to shave him. Every little bit would help keep his identity a secret. She would have to return to the cottage first to get fresh water.

She waited until Alice arrived before returning to the cottage, carrying the basin. She emptied it before entering. Kit was already up, hopping from foot to foot anxiously, awaiting her. "Can I go to help the blacksmith?"

Mercy blinked. He was so excited to do work that it caught her off guard.

"He asked for my help! He said he is working on a

16

sword for one of the bishop's guards. He said I could help pound out the metal because his thumb is hurt! Can I? Can I? Can I?"

Mercy sighed. "Yes. Of course. But remember not to tell Frederick about Joshua. It's a secret."

Kit bobbed his head. "I remember."

"Is Luke going with you?"

Again, a quick nod as he raced for the doorway.

"And remember to take care of the palfrey."

Kit groaned but bobbed his head and ran out into the rising sunshine.

Mercy returned to the barn with fresh water and food. She tried to feed the knight some broth and ground up carrots. It was important he ate to regain his strength. She was on her knees, leaning over him, pressing some smashed carrots between his lips. If he would only swallow some of it, but most of the ground up mush slid from his mouth uneaten.

She sat back, frustrated, her gaze moving over his face. His eyes were closed, his lashes resting against his cheek. One was swollen closed and turning color. His nose was straight. His jaw covered by a full beard. His thick lips were closed, his lower one swollen with a cut marring the rim. What really concerned her was the fact that he hadn't eaten. If he didn't eat or drink, he would perish. He had come so far already, fighting his way through the fever. And she needed him. She scooped up another trencher of the mashed carrots and pressed it against his lips. "Please," she whispered.

Suddenly, he grabbed her wrist and his eye opened to reveal a deep blue orb. "Who are you?" he demanded in a rough voice.

She gasped at his sudden movement, her free hand falling to the dagger in her belt. "My name is Mercy."

He sat up without releasing her wrist. "Where am I?"

"Safe. Do not worry," she said trying to calm him,

pushing her trepidation down.

He looked around the barn slowly and then turned his gaze back to her.

She inhaled slowly. His grip was tight on her arm, but it was his eye that left her breathless. It was intense and piercing. "You were in a fight," she whispered. "I was helping you recover."

Still, he did not release her.

Her gaze swept his face. His jaw was tight, his face battered, but there was something proud and confident in it. "Please. I want to help you. I've been keeping you safe here."

"Where is here?"

"You are in Goodmont. In my barn."

"A barn?" he asked with distaste. "A place where you keep the animals?"

"I thought it better to keep you hidden from the men who attacked you."

He looked at her with a scowl, his gaze slowly moving over her face. He touched his forehead gently. Then, his hand swept by his chin and paused. It slowly moved to his hair, feeling the shortened length with his fingers.

"I had to cut and dye it," Mercy explained quickly. "As a disguise against the men who attacked you."

"I do not need to hide from men."

A grin slipped over her lips and she quickly pushed it away. "You were in no condition to fight them." She eased her wrist from his hold. "Can you eat?"

He glanced down at the floor, the furrow never leaving his brow.

"It's important to keep your strength up."

He turned, attempting to swing his leg from the straw, but winced and clutched his side.

Mercy put her hand on his arm, partly to stop him and partly to help him. "You need to heal."

He shook his head slightly, the scowl deepening.

She quickly picked up the flask from the ground and held it out to him. "At least drink."

He took the flask and drank deeply.

It relieved her to see him follow her instructions. She watched his throat work as he swallowed. He would be hungry soon.

When he handed it back to her, there was gratitude and suspicion in his one open eye. Specks of ale sparkled on his lips.

For a surprising moment, Mercy couldn't look away.

"The fight... I... I don't remember it."

Mercy's eyes widened in shock. "You mean you don't remember who beat you?"

"No." He looked around the floor as if the answer was hidden there. "No. I don't remember... anything before waking up here."

"Nothing?"

He was silent for a moment. Then, he shook his head, his black, chin length locks swaying with the movement. "Nay."

Tremors of apprehension raced down her spine. She nodded, to herself as well as him. "That is common with head injuries. Your memory will return."

He lifted his gaze to her.

For a moment, she saw vulnerability and something else. Something she knew well. Concern. "Worry about recovering. Don't worry about this." She began to collect used cloths and folded them, placing them in a pile. As she worked, she became aware of his stare and turned to him. "You need your strength."

"It is disconcerting not to be able to remember."

She paused her work to look at him.

He stared down at his fist which he was clenching and releasing. "How long have I been here?"

"This is the second day. I think it's a good sign that you have regained consciousness."

"This fight... how did it start?"

"I'm not certain. I wasn't there when it began."

He scowled at his fist. "When I look into my past, I only see darkness."

Her heart leapt in sympathy. He saw darkness in his past and she saw it in her future. She placed a hand over his fist. "It will be alright."

He stared at her hand. "Was I alone?"

"Yes," she said softly. "But you are not any longer."

He slowly lifted his gaze to hers.

Gratitude and something warm simmered in his eyes. She gasped slightly and pulled her hand away. Unnerved by the connection, she gathered the cloth and flask. She began to rise. "I'll bring you some porridge."

He caught her hand. "That sounds good."

His touch was warm and gentle, kind almost. She looked down at his hand wrapped around hers. It engulfed hers in a tenderness that filled her empty soul.

Suddenly, a little whirlwind flew in and she heard a cry, "Let go of my mother!"

She stumbled back when he released her. "Kit!" she called.

The knight had Kit at arm's length, holding Kit's balled hand away from him and the boy's shoulder.

Kit swung his free hand, hitting the knight's arm. "He has a dagger!"

"Kit!" Mercy called, reaching for her son. She grabbed his shoulders firmly, pulling him away from the knight. "He was not hurting me! He doesn't have a dagger! Stop!"

Kit stilled his fight and looked over his shoulder at her, confusion in his blue eyes.

"I'm alright," she insisted.

"I'm not here to harm your mother," the knight said.

Kit straightened.

"Why are you here?" Kit demanded of the knight.

The knight's swollen lip curled in amusement.

"Apparently, to heal."

"Come on, Kit," Mercy said, taking the child's hand. "I was going inside to get some porridge for our guest." Mercy led him out of the barn. When they neared the cottage, she paused. "I told you not to go into the barn."

"You need protection," Kit replied. "He is a strong knight."

Gratitude and fear overwhelmed her. They looked out for each other. She hugged him fiercely. "He's too weak to hurt me." She pulled back to look at him. "Besides. I have my own dagger."

Kit scowled. "What happens when he gets stronger?"

Mercy thought about this. "We'll put him to work mucking out the stalls."

Kit grinned. "As payment for eating our porridge?"

Mercy smiled and messed his curls. "Aye. But you can't attack him like that."

Kit shrugged as he entered the cottage. "Joshua was right behind me. And his dagger is bigger than yours."

Mercy's heart sank. It worried her that Kit felt embolden because of a pretend person. "Will Joshua be here long?"

Kit paused in the doorway to look at her. One of his blonde curls fell into his blue eyes and he brushed it aside. "He goes home at night." He said it matter of factly, as if it was apparent to everyone.

It wasn't time yet to tell him the truth about Joshua. Not yet. He might need Joshua to help him if she couldn't... Her chest tightened and she refused to finish her thought. "You know that Joshua can't really help you, even if he has a big dagger."

"Because he is smaller than me?"

"Because you must depend upon yourself."

"And you."

Again, that tight burning agony filled her chest. She looked down. "And me, yes."

21

"But not that knight."

She glanced back at the barn. It was a shadow against the rising moon. It was strange that she was telling Kit not to trust the knight when all her hopes were with him. "I am hoping we will get to know him enough to trust him, but right now you shouldn't."

"When can I trust him?"

"I'm not certain, but we can start with a bowl of porridge and see him strong." She brushed into the cottage.

Kit skipped behind her. "Can I bring him the porridge?"

Mercy ruffled his hair. "Not yet. I have to get to know him to see whether he is trustworthy." And she hoped he was.

Chapter Three

Richard stretched out his legs slowly. The sunshine shone in through a rotted slat on the side of the barn. At least he could tell the passing of time. It had been one day since he had opened his eyes. He could feel his strength returning. His side was still tender, and his lip still swollen. He could almost see out of his puffy eye; the swelling was easing. The woman, Mercy, had given him a cloth with herbs in it to place over the swelling. It seemed to be helping.

It was his head he was worried about. Last night, pain had pierced through his mind like a sword. He could barely sleep. Now, he was tired but wanted to rise and test his mobility. He vowed he would stand today. He was no cripple to be lying in a barn and be tended to. He was a knight and had had worse than a sound beating. Startled, he realized that he *was* a knight. Some part of his memory was still there. Perhaps Mercy was right, and all his memory would return.

When he heard movement, he glanced at the door.

"I'm not going in when he is awake," a voice said in a hushed tone, but not hushed enough that he did not hear.

"I will tend him." He knew that voice. Mercy.

"I don't like you treating him alone."

"I treat many men alone."

"They are villagers. All of whom we know."

"Then come in with me." The door opened and Mercy entered, carrying a bucket of water.

He grinned. He was beginning to really like her. He felt a strange rush of anticipation when he knew she was coming. Her presence made his pain tolerable.

He caught sight of an elderly woman standing with her arms crossed outside of the door. "I'll be right here…"

The door closed on her words.

"That's two," he greeted as Mercy dropped to her knees at his side.

She lifted her blue eyes to his. "Two?"

"Two people who have warned you about me."

Confusion marred her brow.

"The little boy and the woman," he clarified.

She lifted her eyebrows in understanding and then brushed the thought aside with a wave of her hand. She took a cloth from the pile she carried in after setting the two basins on the ground.

"You don't think I'm a threat?"

She looked him in the eye. "Are you?" She looked doubtful.

He took offense and drew himself up. "At times."

She smiled and turned to the basin. She gently dipped the cloth into the water and wrung it out.

He scowled. "I can be," he insisted.

"I'll keep that in mind."

He sank back against the wall and lifted his knee. Agony flared up from his stomach, and he winced, even though he tried to hide it.

She paused, seeing the grimace. "How is your head?"

He lifted his hand to touch his forehead. "It will do."

Mercy put a hand on her waist and cocked her head to the side. "It will only help your recovery and my ministrations if you tell the truth. There's no need for you to feel threatened by me."

"Threatened?" he asked in disbelief. He didn't find women threatening.

"I've come across this before. Men do not want to feel inferior to women, so they push aside their aches and lie about their condition. And then they die, or sometimes have a leg cut off."

"How long have you been a physician?"

A grin touched her lips as she removed a cloth from a cut on his arm. "I'm not a physician. My husband was."

He held his arm out for her. "Was? Where is he now? Perhaps he can treat me."

Mercy sat back on her heels. "I should be insulted, but I'm not. I'm sure Dean would have treated you if he could. He passed away."

"I'm sorry."

Mercy nodded. "You and the entire village, I'm sure."

Richard scowled. "I meant no disrespect."

She shook her head and dabbed at the cut. "I learned a lot from him, but I'm no physician. Still, I'm the best the village has. I have taken his place in their eyes." She sat back without replacing the cloth.

"How long ago did he die?"

"Two years. He fell ill and never recovered. But you are avoiding the question. How is your head?"

"It hurts at times. But it is nothing I cannot endure."

Mercy grinned. "I'm sure." Her smile faded. "Have you remembered anything further?"

He shook his head. "No. I try, but I can't."

"Do you remember anything? Your name? Where you came from?"

"Sometimes I feel as if it is just there, behind the fog, but I can't find it. Have you ever forgotten a word? It's like that. I know it, but I can't...seem to find it."

"Relax," she said softly. "It will come back. But until

25

then, we must call you something."

"Eoos." The word came to him and he didn't know from where and he didn't know if that was his name or not. But it was familiar.

"Eoos?" Mercy repeated, baffled.

He nodded. Yes. The word was so familiar that it must be his name.

"Eoos," she seemed to roll the word around as if tasting it. Then, nodded. She lifted her gaze to his. A ray of sunlight splashed across her eyes making them sparkle. She was beautiful, he suddenly realized, and was shocked by his realization.

She leaned forward and brushed her fingers against one of the bruises on his stomach.

He jumped as tingles danced through his torso.

"Does that hurt?"

He shook his head. No. It did not hurt at all. Her touch was like magic, strangely sensual. Calming and arousing at the same time. As she continued touching him, he cleared his throat. He needed to get his mind off her closeness, her very alluring smell. "Do you know anything about my past? Who I am or whenst I come?"

She moved her fingers to another bruise, tenderly pressing against it. "I know of no man named Eoos."

He had thought that perchance he had come from Goodmont, but apparently that was not the case. "Do you know anything of me?"

"I know you were beaten at the inn."

"Do you know why?"

Her concentration centered on his stomach, perhaps too much so. She leaned in close to peel a cloth from one of the cuts on his torso.

One of her brown locks fell forward and brushed against his skin, sending tremors through his body. Gods blood! How much more agonizing torture could she put him through?

She set the cloth aside and reached for a flask. Then she shook her head.

"Do you know who did it?" he asked in a husky voice.

"Aye," she said, pouring cool liquid over the wound.

He winced and stiffened, but the burning subsided.

"I would not approach them until you get your strength back." She put a fresh cloth over the cut.

Wise advice. Suddenly, pain erupted through his cloudy mind and the fog seemed to part. He was in a room, looking up through a crowd of faces as she came toward him. Mercy. And then, he remembered the angel who had saved him. "It was you."

She lifted her confused gaze to lock with his.

He reached out and captured her hand, partly to prevent her from turning away, partly to hold onto something through the pain. "Why? Why did you stop them?"

"They would have killed you. I didn't think that was a sin the men of this village needed to harbor in their souls." She looked at him again with a strange contemplative expression before pulling her hand away and turning to collect her cloth. "A few more days of rest and you should be well enough to be on your feet. I left a blade and basin of water for you to shave with. If you need help, I can help you when I return."

The pain in his mind dulled and faded. He didn't want her to leave. Not yet. "Mercy!"

She turned to him.

His gaze swept over her face. So beautiful. Her hair was pulled back in a coif, strands of dark curls hanging around her oval shaped face. Her blue eyes lit his soul like the sun. Her lips were full and tempting. Lord, he wanted to kiss her.

Mercy cocked her head to the side, her eyes narrowing slightly.

Richard's heart pounded. He wanted to reach out and touch her. He wanted to pull her against him and kiss her deeply. Instead, he just sat.

She stood, holding the basin before her. "You are welcome to stay until you can ride." She turned away and headed for the door.

"I don't believe that I thanked you. For everything."

She turned to him; her shapely lips turned up at the corners in a grin.

It was as though he caught his breath, as though he were holding his breath. He couldn't explain the strange sensation that suddenly engulfed him.

"No. You didn't." She continued out of the barn.

Mercy eased the door closed behind her, holding the basin of water and some soiled cloth.

"What did he say?" Abbey pushed herself from the side of the barn. "Will he help us?"

"Shh," Mercy warned, glancing back at the barn and then at Abbey. "Where's Alice?"

"Inside."

"I didn't ask him. It's too early. He's still recovering."

Abbey's face fell in worry. "I don't have much time. They'll come for Luke in two days." She grabbed Mercy's arm, and water sloshed over the side of the basin onto the dirt at her feet. "I don't want to give my baby up."

"I know," Mercy whispered. And she did. But she didn't know what else to do. The men of the village refused to stand against the bishop.

"The bishop comes with two guards every time. I can't fight them alone." Abbey shook her head.

"Follow the plan. Just say no to the bishop."

Abbey nodded, but she looked fearful. "It's not right. The bishop takes the boys, and we never see them again. We don't know what he does with them. I won't give Luke up.

Not even to do God's work."

Mercy chewed thoughtfully on her lower lip. She wasn't certain that Abbey was strong enough to deny the bishop. "Have you considered running?"

"Running?"

"Leaving the village."

"Where would I go? A woman and a child alone on the road?" Abbey shook her head. "I couldn't do that."

Kit and another boy with dark hair ran past them.

"Don't forget the horse!" Mercy called after Kit.

The boys giggled as they disappeared into the field of long stalks.

Mercy started across the yard toward the cottage. The clouds had covered the sun and a cool breeze touched her cheeks. She caught a glimpse of Kit and Luke through the crops as they jumped up and down to scare the birds. So innocent. She wished they could just be boys and not have to worry about the bishop and being torn away from their families.

Mercy and Abbey had made it halfway across the yard, when she heard conversation coming from the road. Low conversation. She glanced toward the road to see Simon the farmer and Lief the town's rat catcher, walking toward her. The bald spot on Simon's head shone in the sunlight. He used a hoe to aid him in walking, even though he didn't need it. Lief was younger than Simon, with brown hair that was plastered to his head.

She quickly handed the basin to Abbey. "Bring this inside."

"I'm not leaving you. You know what they want."

Mercy wiped her hands on her brown skirt and approached the men as tingles of trepidation shivered down her spine. "Good day!"

The men stopped talking and walked up to her. Lief pushed his brown hair flat with his hand as he approached.

Mercy realized what Abbey was speaking of. Dread

welled up inside her. She mentally counted the day and realized with growing alarm that it was Friday. She was to have an answer for Lief. She should have told him no immediately when he asked to marry her, but she was so tired she just wanted to get home. She had promised to have an answer for him by...today.

"I've come for your answer," Lief said.

"And I'm here as a witness," Simon added.

Abbey grumbled something unintelligible about Simon.

Mercy drew in a deep breath. She didn't want to hurt Lief but had no intention of marrying him. He could not protect Kit. And that would be the only reason she would marry again.

"Lief," she started quietly. "I appreciate your offer –"

"It's dangerous out here on the fringe of the village all by yourself," Simon said, cutting her off. He glanced at the field and then the cottage. "How long before a brigand comes and steals your horse?"

"Walter visits to make sure Kit and I are safe."

"As do I," Abbey added.

"And what good would you be against brigands?" Simon demanded of Abbey in a sharp tone. "Walter is an old man. He is no deterrent to thieves. Now, Lief here is strong and fit."

Not for a sword, Mercy wanted to say, but kept silent. She began to shake her head.

"Think on it, girl," Simon warned. "You are in no position to be alone."

Mercy narrowed her eyes at Simon. "Shouldn't you be harvesting your crops?"

Simon scratched his stringy brown hair. "Amelia is working the fields."

"Your wife?" Mercy gasped. Simon was a lazy man, prone to letting others do his work. Poor Amelia. "Alone? Aren't you worried about thieves coming to rob you?"

Simon grimaced in distaste.

"You should help her," Mercy advised.

"You should learn your place. Women don't tell men what they should be doing. That has always been your fault. That husband of yours shoulda beat some sense into you instead of letting you do whatever you like."

Mercy's lips tightened. She looked at Lief. "I'm sorry, Lief. I appreciate your offer of marriage and protection, but you are not the man for me."

Lief scowled in disappointment but bobbed his head.

Mercy regretted being harsh with him. Simon was the one her anger and impatience should be aimed at.

"You'll regret this," Simon promised.

"Are you threatening me?"

"Those brigands will come and pull up your skirts and have their way with you. You'd probably like it."

"Get off my lands."

Simon stepped toward her. "A woman has no right to own lands. It's not natural."

"And yet I do."

Lief grabbed his arm, but Simon yanked it away.

"Simon," Lief warned. "She doesn't want me. It is her right."

"Her right?" Simon said. "Someone shoulda taught her the proper place for a woman." He grabbed her shoulders.

"Momma!" Kit cried from the edge of the field where he and Luke were watching. He began racing forward across the yard.

Abbey shrunk back in fear.

"Stay there, Kit!" Mercy ordered with a firm voice that stopped Kit in his tracks. She pulled the dagger from her belt and pressed the tip against Simon's stomach. She tried to remain calm even though her heart raced. "Get your hands off of me."

For a moment, everything froze. Simon's angry eyes glared into hers. His fingers tightened over her shoulders.

Would she stab him? Could she do it when all her training was to save and help the villagers?

Simon pushed her back. "You're not worth it." He spat on the ground and took a step backward.

Kit raced up and hugged her leg.

Mercy stood for a long moment, shaken. She didn't realize she was holding her breath until she inhaled deeply and let it out slowly. As she watched Simon and Lief move off down the road, Simon cussing all the way, she slowly lowered her arm holding the dagger. If Simon had his way, she would be married off to his friend and they would be sitting in the house drinking ale while she and Kit worked the fields. She looked down at Kit, resting a hand on his blonde curls. "I'm fine, Kit," she whispered.

"Are you alright?" Abbey asked.

Mercy nodded. Simon was right about one thing. She did need protection. She and Kit both. As she turned toward the cottage, she saw the barn door swing shut.

Chapter Four

Mercy stared at the boys as they slept on the straw mattress tucked in the corner. So peaceful, not a care in the world. She was envious.

Abbey clutched Mercy's hand tightly across the table. "Simon is not going to like that you rejected Lief."

Mercy squeezed her hand. "Nor that I pulled a dagger on him."

Abbey giggled softly. "That was a sight!" She grunted. "Serves him right. I wish I had the courage to draw a dagger on him. And on all the rest of those cowards in the village." She leaned forward. "Do you really think the knight will defend us?"

Mercy cast a glance across the room toward the door and the barn beyond. "He doesn't remember who he is. Or what he's done. I should have told him that he killed the Archbishop."

Abbey sat back. "What good would it have done?"

"It's not right to keep his identity a secret. He deserves to know."

Abbey leaned forward again. "Tell him."

"Tell him what? What he's done?" Abbey nodded and

33

Mercy continued, "And then what?"

"He can stand against the bishop. He can defend us. Protect the children. Lord knows the men of Goodmont won't do it. We need a man of honor!"

Mercy raised her eyebrows in surprise. "He killed the Archbishop. He is *not* a man of honor."

"He stood up to the Archbishop of Canterbury."

"He *killed* the Archbishop of Canterbury."

"Maybe he should kill Bishop –"

"Don't say it."

"You're thinking it. I am too. We've talked about it. It's the only way."

Mercy sighed softly. "Another bishop will be assigned to take his place. He might take our children, too."

"And he might not. Do you really believe the orders come from above the bishop to steal our children? What would the church want with young boys?"

Mercy didn't know. She didn't know what the bishop did with the children.

"Bishop Devdan rips the children away from their mothers, their families. We never see them again. Something is very wrong with that." Abbey shook her head. "The knight is already excommunicated. Surely, he would kill a man of the cloth again to save my boy, to save an innocent child."

Mercy knew what Abbey was going through. She was feeling the same thing. Desperation. She had to save Kit. She had to find a way. They had talked quietly about killing the bishop previously. It was desperation. They would never do it. It was a sin. But could a man who was already guilty of such a crime do it? Still, Mercy was against killing. She was a healer. "The knight cannot even stand. How would he fight the bishop's men?" There had to be another way. "We can hide Luke."

"They'll look for him. And Simon will help. You know he will."

"We can hide him in the forest. Deep in the forest. No one would find him!"

"Forever?" Abbey shook her head. "No. I would have to leave him alone and I wouldn't do that."

"You could hide him in our barn."

Abbey looked grateful, but she shook her head. "If Simon or the others found out, you would be in trouble. I wouldn't do that to you." She tightened her hand around Mercy's. "Kit's time is coming, too."

Mercy's heart skipped a beat. Yes, they would come for Kit a week after Luke. If they couldn't save Luke, how could she hope they would save Kit?

Mercy arrived for the meeting the village men held before every child turned five summers. She followed Walter and Abbey inside the inn. It was crowded, every seat taken by a man from the village. She acknowledged Frederick the blacksmith, with a nod, and Roger the farmer. She passed Simon without a glance. Walter led them to three chairs at a table in the back. Bartholomew, the innkeeper, lounged against one of the walls, his face twisted in a grimace.

Mercy and Abbey were the only women in the room, something Mercy had grown used to since Dean had died. Only landowners were allowed in these meetings.

"I will have a full basket of onions to give the bishop," Roger was saying.

"That's not going to appease him," one of the other men said.

"Do you think he wants roots?" Simon demanded with contempt. "He wants the children."

Mercy had just sat and added, "We should stand against him."

Everyone looked at her.

"Of course, she would say that!" Simon said pointing to her. "The bishop is taking her boy at the next full moon!"

Mercy ground her teeth. "I said that last month and the month before."

"How can we stand against the church?" Roger asked from his spot at a table near the doorway.

"He has armed men that do his bidding," someone added. "I don't want to end up in the dungeon."

"I have a family to think about," another said.

"We're just villagers, not fighters."

This was the same meeting they had every time a child turned five. The men made excuses and were as useless as ever. Rage boiled inside of Mercy. She slapped her hands on the table as desperation swelled over her. "He is taking our children! Not our crops, not our land. Our boys!"

Quiet murmuring followed her statement.

"How can you let him do this?"

"How can we stop him?" Roger asked.

Mercy hesitated. She saw the conflict in the men's eyes. She saw the reluctance. Not only were they incapable of standing up to the bishop, but they didn't have the means. They could not fight the bishop's wealth nor the power of his armed men. How could she ask them to? She glanced at Abbey. Tearful fear welled in Abbey's dark eyes. How could she not ask the men to fight for their children? "We have to do something."

"We can try to appease him with offerings," Thomas suggested.

"The children are our offering. We don't know what he does with them. We don't know where they go," Roger said with agony in his voice. "He doesn't want anything else."

He had lost a boy six months ago. Given up his baby. He had three other daughters and a wife he had to look after. He justified it as his son's duty.

"There is something that might appease him," Walter

mumbled.

Mercy looked at him, but he would not meet her eye. He stared down at the wooden table before them, his finger tracing the path of the grain.

"The knight," Walter announced.

Shock raced through Mercy followed by fear. Why wouldn't he have asked her first?

"Yes!" Simon agreed.

Mercy swallowed hard. Walter looked at her. She implored him with her eyes, shaking her head just a little.

Everyone looked at Mercy. They all knew she had him. Agony twisted her heart. No. She needed him. He was her only hope to save Kit. He just needed time to heal. "How do we know the bishop won't still take Luke? And Kit? How do we know that giving up the knight will be the end of it?"

"We don't. But we have no other option," Simon grumbled.

"We can stand up to him! Tell him no. As a village. Together. He can't have our children!"

"It's easy for you to say! Your boy is almost five summers!"

The room exploded in protests and arguments.

"We can't stand against the bishop! He is the church!"

"Think of God's wrath!"

"I have a family!"

She watched the exchange, as if from afar. Arguing, shouting. She would not give Eoos up. "He escaped," she whispered.

The room quieted. Walter looked at her. Abbey stared at her, mouth agape.

"What did you say?" Simon demanded.

"He escaped," she said in a louder voice. "The night Walter brought him to my barn. You had beaten him so badly I didn't think he could move. I didn't bind him. I didn't think he would have the strength to leave. When I checked in the morning, he was gone."

"We should look for him," Thomas said. "If we can find him soon, perhaps we could exchange him for Luke."

Abbey scowled fiercely at Mercy.

Mercy retook her seat, quietly.

"Bart," Simon called. "You were the one to recognize him. Tell them what the knight looks like so we can go after him."

Bartholomew rubbed his stomach. "He is tall, taller than anyone in this room. He has long brown hair, a beard, and icy blue eyes. He can wield a sword savagely."

"That's the man we fought in the inn," Simon nodded in recollection. "Remember how he fought back? Remember it took all of us to overpower him?"

Mercy locked eyes with Abbey. She couldn't give him up. He would help them, he must! She had already disguised him so the village men wouldn't find him. She wanted to run home to make sure he was safe. But she knew if she left now, it would be as good as admitting guilt.

"He is called the brute because he is," Bartholomew continued. "He takes what he wants because he can. He doesn't care for or have any compassion for anyone but himself."

She scowled in confusion. "That's not what I saw when I found you attacking him. You had him on the floor, beating him. He wasn't fighting back," Mercy said. She looked at Bartholomew. Maybe they had the wrong man. "Are you sure the man you beat that night was the brute?"

Bart nodded. "I saw him once when I was in Essex. I know him."

"We need to find him," Simon grumbled. "Beaten like that, he couldn't have gotten far."

Bart agreed with a nod. "He is a danger to the village. We should tell the bishop what happened."

"It doesn't matter now. He's gone."

"It might bring more of the bishop's wrath down on the village if he knew we had the brute and he got away,"

Thomas commented.

"But we should warn the bishop," someone said.

"Pah. The bishop is well protected. The village is not. I think –"

The conversation faded into the background as Mercy thought of Eoos, the brute. He was no danger to them. She had to convince him to help them. Somehow. She swiveled her stare to Abbey. Abbey stared hard at her. There was a scowl of displeasure and disagreement on her brow.

"We'll search for the knight," Simon said. "We have a day to find him. If we do, we can exchange him for Luke."

"It won't work," Mercy whispered. But no one heard her.

The men began making plans to search for a man that was hidden in Mercy's barn. For a man too weak to fight back. They didn't even know if giving him to the bishop in exchange for Luke would work!

She looked at Abbey. She was visibly shaking. Hot, angry desperation filled her; she was slowly shaking her head.

As the meeting ended, the men stood and filed toward the exit, nodding in approval and satisfaction at their plan. Simon crossed through the men to stop before Abbey.

"We'll find that knight and save your boy," he said.

Mercy cast a glance at Abbey. The bishop was coming to take Luke in one day. One day. She wasn't certain that Abbey had the strength to stand up to the bishop. She didn't have confidence in their plan. They needed more.

Chapter Five

The next day, Mercy made her rounds. The blacksmith seemed to be healing nicely, and she gave the wife of Daniel the farmer, who was sick with stomach pains, some wormwood and mint to mix in her food.

On her way back home, her mind wandered to Eoos. She had to protect him so he could recover. And, in return, she hoped he could help them with the bishop. She was hoping he could fight off the bishop's men and save the children. But she knew this wouldn't be enough. The bishop would bring more men. Eoos would be taken as well as Kit. Hopeless despair swirled inside her. Her mind continued to return to the fact that he had killed the Archbishop. Would asking him to kill Bishop Devdan be enough to solve the problem? To save the children?

As she continued home, lost in thought, it took a moment for her to realize someone was calling her. She turned and saw Walter approaching her. He kicked up little puffs of dirt as he hurried toward her. Mercy smiled in greeting but saw the seriousness etched in his brow. "Is everyone alright?"

He grabbed her arm. "Simon is furious you didn't

accept Lief's proposal."

Mercy grimaced and opened her mouth to respond.

Walter continued, "He is going to search your home for the knight. He is riding to your place now."

Tingles of trepidation danced along her spine. He had not finished the words when Mercy spun and raced for home. Her heart pounded as her feet stomped the dirt in her hurry. She cut through Daniel's wheat field. The branch from a weed snagged her dress. She reached down to rip it away when its sharp tip tore her skirt. She barely stopped.

He couldn't take Eoos! Her mind continued to repeat no, no, no. Over and over. As she rounded a copse of trees separating Daniel's field from her land, her cottage came into view. It looked so peaceful, as if it were just another day.

Then, she heard Kit's cry.

Her heart lurched and she forced herself to go faster. If Simon hurt Kit, if he touched him…

She hurried forward, rounding the cottage. Kit was on the ground near the barn, holding his cheek and looking up at Simon.

Rage filled Mercy, but before she could act, the door to the barn swung open and Eoos exploded from within like a dark storm cloud. He lifted his fist and delivered a solid blow to Simon's jaw.

A strangled sound issued from her lips as she ran across the road and threw herself over Kit to protect him, her eyes sweeping her child for injury. His cheek was red, but it seemed to be his only injury.

She locked eyes with Simon who was in the dirt just feet from them. His eyes were wide in disbelief as they swiveled to Eoos towering above him.

"If you feel the need to hit a child again, seek me out first," Eoos snarled between clenched teeth.

Mercy shot to her feet, laying a hand on his shirtless arm. Eoos looked at her, and when their gazes met, she saw the reined fury snapping in his blue eyes. Then, she spun on Simon. "How dare you strike my son?" she demanded of Simon. "I will take this up with the magistrate."

Simon climbed to his feet; a head shorter than Eoos. He stared at Eoos, his lips twitching in hatred. "Who is this?"

The words came naturally to Mercy. "This is my cousin, Eoos. He's come to offer me and Kit the protection you said we need."

Simon narrowed his eyes in disbelief. "He looks like that knight."

"He looks nothing like that knight!" She glanced at Eoos and was glad he had shaved his beard. She looked back at Simon. "I'm telling you, this isn't the knight." She was furious. Furious that Simon had struck Kit. Furious that she didn't realize the threat Simon presented. "I already told you the knight *escaped*." Beside her, she felt Eoos's fist clench. She squeezed his arm in a warning to stay silent. "Would you tell the bishop that? Would you tell him how you let the knight escape?"

Simon seemed to think about this. He spit on the ground. "An excommunicated knight. We should have killed him when we had the chance."

"Murder is a sin."

Simon looked at Eoos carefully, his eyes narrowed again. "He has the same marks as a man who was in a fight at the inn would have."

"Aye," Mercy said. "They are bruises one gets in a common fight. Some brigands came last night. He fought them off."

Simon's eyes narrowed further in doubt.

"Just like you said they would. We were lucky Eoos was here."

Simon grimaced. He looked at Mercy. "You should have married Lief." He began to back away.

Mercy felt a swirling of dread and relief. She had lied to Simon to protect Eoos. And she would do it again to save him. She released his arm and stepped after Simon. "You are not welcomed here, Simon."

"I never was."

Eoos stepped past her.

Simon quickened his pace down the road and off her lands.

Mercy dropped to her knees at Kit's side. She took his face in her hands, examining his cheek. A hot red handprint was appearing on his tender skin. "Are you alright?"

Kit wrapped his arms about her, and she hugged him fiercely.

"What were you doing?" Mercy whispered to him. "Why did he hit you?"

"I was telling him to stay away from our barn," Kit said, pressing his face into her shoulder. "That he couldn't go in. He didn't like that."

Mercy squeezed Kit tightly. She picked Kit up and turned to Eoos. In the light of day, he looked worse. His eye was swollen closed and turning colors, his lip puffed up. His cheek was swollen. And still, he had protected her son. Overwhelming gratitude consumed her. "Thank you."

He nodded his head before wincing and grasping his stomach.

"You shouldn't be on your feet," Mercy advised.

"I thought it was the right thing to do."

Her heart melted. She was so grateful to him. "It was," she whispered, stroking Kit's head.

He nodded. "Am I truly your cousin?"

She smiled. "No. I made that up so he wouldn't recognize you from the inn."

"Then I am the knight who was excommunicated."

She froze. She should tell him the truth. She should tell him what he had done.

Kit looked at her. "You lied?"

She was lying about a good many things. And she didn't like it. Not one bit. She considered Richard to be dishonorable, yet she was the one telling shameful lies. "I did it to protect Eoos."

Kit rubbed his cheek. "At least your lie didn't hurt as much as Simon's hit."

It could hurt worse, she knew, if the bishop found out. She kissed his cheek and began to carry Kit across the yard to the cottage. She was so thankful Eoos was there to protect Kit. She paused and turned back to Eoos. "Come inside. Warm yourself by the fire."

Eoos paused and glanced at the barn. Then, he nodded and followed her.

Eoos ducked his head beneath the door frame as he swiped aside the cloth acting as a door and entered. He didn't like that this thin fabric was the only thing separating Mercy and her son from the outside. His gaze swept the room.

Near the far wall, a fire burned in the hearth and a pot hung over it. A chicken raced across his feet, flapping its wings. Tucked into a corner of the room was a straw mattress big enough for Mercy and her boy. There was a table and two chairs near the hearth, and a thin elderly woman sat in one of them. When she saw them, she rubbed the back of her neck anxiously. "What happened?"

Mercy put Kit down and the boy raced after the chicken. "Simon wanted to have words with Eoos."

The elderly woman's eyes slid to Eoos, and a look of terror crossed her face.

Mercy lay a hand on her wrist. "Eoos protected Kit."

The woman's gaze slid to the boy. "Is he alright? What did Simon do?"

"He'll be fine. Thanks to Eoos." Both women turned and looked at him.

Eoos felt a rush of warmth move up his face. "It was nothing," he stated, but he was happy to help Mercy. His stare shifted to her and their gazes locked. Something protective and appreciative bubbled inside him.

Kit paused with the chicken in his arms and elaborated. "He punched Simon in the face! One punch knocked Simon to the ground."

Mercy nodded at the woman's shocked expression.

"Do you think that made matters worse?" the woman asked.

"He has no right to strike a child," Eoos defended.

Again, both women looked at him.

Eoos lifted his chin stubbornly.

Mercy looked at the woman again. "I told him Eoos was my cousin."

The woman's eyebrows shot up and her gaze locked on Eoos. "I'll tell Walter."

"I would like to know why I was excommunicated," Eoos stated.

Time seemed to stop. The two women froze for a long moment, saying nothing but staring at him. Then they looked at each other. He was certain they knew something. And then, the moment passed.

"Here, Alice!" Kit held the chicken out to her.

"Would you like some porridge?" Mercy asked Eoos as she stepped past the woman.

It was as if he had never commented. As if the statement never existed. "Yes. Thank you."

Unease spread through him. He stepped up to Mercy as she took a trencher and scooped porridge out of the pot. He opened his mouth to ask about the excommunication again when the fire below the pot caught his attention. Orange and red tongues flicked over the sides of the thick logs beneath the black pot.

Suddenly, he began to see something else. A different fire in a different hearth. His mind superimposed the memory over the real fire. He was confused at first as to what was happening. And then, the sharp pain exploded through his mind. He staggered, putting a hand to his forehead.

He heard someone calling. He felt hands on him, but he wasn't sure whose hands they were.

"Eoos!"

Mercy's call snapped him from the memory. The sharp pain receded.

Mercy stood over him. Confused, he realized he was sitting in a chair. Alice stood near a pen with other chickens, holding the one Kit gave her. Kit stood behind his mother, staring in alarm. But it was Mercy's furrowed brow, her fear, that brought him back to the present.

"A memory," he said quietly.

She put her hand against his forehead. "Were you in pain?"

He shook his head stubbornly. "Nothing I couldn't handle."

She pulled her hand away from his head. "No fever." She stared at him with concern. "Does your head hurt?"

"No longer. Only when I remember." He glanced over her shoulder at the boy. "It is nothing. I am fine."

Kit looked at him doubtfully. "Sometimes I stub my toe and it hurts, but then the pain goes away. Was it like that?"

Eoos nodded.

"What did you remember?" Mercy asked.

He glanced toward the hearth. "The fire. I saw other flames in a different hearth."

"Perhaps the hearth at the inn," Alice offered.

"I wouldn't know. But I'd like to see the inn I was attacked in. It could bring back more memories."

Mercy glanced at Alice.

For a moment, Eoos swore there was alarm in Alice's wide eyes.

Mercy shook her head. "You're still recovering. I don't

think it's wise."

Eoos scowled. "I want to know who I am. I want my memories back."

"It could be dangerous. We should wait until you are stronger."

Eoos shook his head. "We will go. Soon."

Mercy sighed softly and then nodded. "Yes. Of course. You should rest now, though. I will take you tomorrow afternoon."

Eoos agreed with a nod.

"Are you sure you're ready for more memories?" she asked with a worried frown.

Eoos was touched by her worry. Or was there more to why she didn't want him thinking of his memories? "Yes."

"I mean... the pain you were in just now...when you remembered."

"I am willing to submit to the pain if it brings back my past."

Alice snorted as she crossed the room to the hearth. "Some pasts are best forgotten."

Eoos frowned. "Do you know my past?"

Her eyes rounded in terror. "No. No. I know nothing."

Eoos knew a lie when he heard one. This woman knew more than she was saying. The tension in the room strung tight. What were they hiding? Were they protecting him? Or were they protecting someone else? Either way, they were not going to tell him, but he would find out soon enough.

"It will be alright," Mercy said. "You'll remember everything, I'm certain. For now, you need to eat and regain your strength."

He looked at the trencher and pulled it over to him, beginning to eat the porridge.

Mercy handed Kit a trencher of porridge. The boy hopped from one foot to the other as he ate. When he was almost finished, Mercy asked, "Kit, have you fed the horses?"

Kit's eyes widened as he licked his fingers. He puffed out his lower lip and rubbed his cheek. "I was on my way when Simon came."

Mercy turned to regard him with a suspicious gaze.

Kit sighed and dropped his hand. "I'll do it now." He kicked at a pebble and headed for the doorway. Suddenly, he stopped and looked at Eoos. "If you think it's okay, maybe I can show Eoos his horse!"

Eoos stood. "I have a horse?"

Mercy grinned. "That's a good idea, Kit. I need to help Alice clean up. As soon as I am finished, I will come to the barn." She looked at her son. "Kit, if anything happens to Eoos, come and get me."

Kit bobbed his head, a strand of hair falling into his eyes.

Eoos took two large strides and was at the child's side.

"The worst job is mucking out the stalls," Kit said as they left the cottage. "But I like to be around the horses." He led the way across the yard toward the barn and behind it. "We're lucky. None of the other villagers have a barn, but sometimes my mom houses sick animals there."

"She treats animals as well as people?" Eoos asked, following the child. He took one step to every three the boy took.

"Aye. There was one time when a goat was having a baby and the baby died inside the mother. It was gross. But mom saved the goat momma." The child rounded the back of the barn. A beautiful horse was tied to a wooden beam. It whinnied and tossed its dark head.

Eoos stopped, staring at the palfrey. "This is my horse?"

Kit nodded. He walked up to the horse and patted its neck. "We didn't know what his name was, so I named him Pounder because he stomps the ground a lot." Kit picked up the bucket near the side of the barn.

Eoos stared, trying desperately to remember. But nothing came. Only empty memories swirled in his mind.

"Come on, Eoos."

The horse whinnied and tossed its head.

Eoos stepped closer to the horse. "He's beautiful." He stretched out his hand and the horse pushed its nose against his palm.

"He remembers you," Kit said.

A strange longing rose in Eoos as he ran his hand along the horse's nose. He wanted to remember. He focused, but nothing came to him. He scowled, frustrated.

"We have to get the grain, Eoos."

The horse whinnied and tossed its head again.

Eoos nodded and backed away from the animal, following Kit into the barn.

Kit moved to the rear of the structure and disappeared inside one of the stalls. As Eoos followed, a reflected light caught his attention and he glanced into one of the stalls. A full set of plate armor lay on the ground. "What is this?"

Kit looked out from the last stall. "Your armor." He hurried over to Eoos. "It's amazing, isn't it?"

"It shouldn't be on the ground, it will rust." As soon as the words left his mouth, he wondered how he knew that. But there was more. "The suit needs to be cleaned and set upright, off the ground."

"I don't know how to clean it or I would have," Kit admitted.

"Like this." Eoos moved into the stall. He grabbed a cloth laying over the side wall and picked up the helmet from the ground. He stared at it for a long time, trying to remember how he knew to clean it. He ran the cloth over the dirt on the metal helmet, and it came away. "It needs to be cleaned immediately because you can't use water on it." He scrubbed the dirt from the base and moved upward. Again, he paused to stare at it. As a knight, wouldn't he remember his own helmet?

Kit came to his side with a cloth in his hand. "You just scrub?"

Eoos nodded and moved the cloth back and forth over the metal.

Kit took one of the gauntlets in his small hand and started working on it.

"It's hard work to clean armor," Eoos said.

"I would spend all night cleaning it if I could. Not too many knights come through here. Well, except for the Bishop's men. And Mom told me to stay away from them."

Bishop's men? "Doesn't the village have a lord? What about his men?"

"Naw. The bishop is in charge here. He protects the village. Well, everyone except for the children."

Eoos looked at the small boy. The child put all his effort and concentration into cleaning the gauntlet. "Why doesn't the bishop protect children? It would seem to me that children and women need the most protecting."

Kit pursed his lips. "Maybe. But that's not how the bishop sees it. I had a friend named Rafe, we played together a lot when I was little. Sometimes, we played knights." He smiled, but slowly his grin faded. "And then, his time came and I never saw him again."

"His time?"

Kit nodded. "Five summers."

"What happened to him?"

"The bishop took him."

Eoos scowled in confusion. "Where did the bishop take him?"

"I don't know. I never saw him again." Kit scrubbed harder.

Eoos watched the boy. His innocent brow was marred by a frown. He seemed so vulnerable.

"It is Luke's time tomorrow. The bishop will come for him."

Eoos allowed the child to speak. It didn't make sense to

him. Why take the children?

"I don't tell Mom, but I'm afraid sometimes."

Eoos dropped to one knee to be eye-level with Kit. He put a hand on the boy's shoulder. "Why?"

"I'm almost five summers."

Trepidation snaked through Eoos. He was not certain he was understanding the boy. "The bishop will take you?"

Kit nodded without looking at him.

"Away from your mother?"

Another nod. "I don't want to go. I want to stay with Mum." His voice became thick and his lower lip puffed out.

"I'm sure your mother will not let you go."

He looked up at Eoos with tears in his large eyes. "She won't be able to stop him. No one can."

His misery and fear tugged at Eoos's heart. "I'll do everything I can to help. Don't worry, Kit. If you don't want to go, you won't go."

Kit threw his arms around Eoos.

Startled, Eoos resisted for a moment and then allowed himself to sink into the hug.

Chapter Six

Usually, the mornings were quiet. Eoos was pulling on his boots when he heard movement in the barn. He paused, listening. Was it that farmer returning?

Rustling came from the stall beside him. As he stood, he heard the ping of metal against metal. Slowly, he looked around the wall.

Kit sat on the ground, the breastplate on his lap. He held a cloth and was scrubbing vigorously with so much concentration that he didn't hear Eoos enter.

Eoos stood for a moment. The armor was already cleaned. Kit had done a thorough job with it earlier. He picked up the left cuisses and a cloth and sat opposite of Kit. He knew something was bothering the boy.

The two worked in silence.

Eoos focused on scrubbing the armor, watching Kit's reflection in the smooth polished metal. "Where's your Mom?"

"In the village," he said with a pout.

Eoos didn't look up. "It's early."

Kit scowled. "It's Luke's day. She went to help his Mom."

Eoos paused and looked up at the boy.

"It's his turn to go with the bishop," Kit said softly. "I'll never see him again."

Understanding dawned in Eoos. It was what Kit was so fearful of. He had to see it. He had to understand what happened. He stood. "Be brave, Kit."

Kit looked up at him. "Where are you going?"

"To see for myself."

Mercy reluctantly made her way into the village. She knew the routine too well. The street was crowded with men and few women from the village. There were no children, except for the sacrifice. Mercy immediately saw Abbey standing before the Wolf's inn. Bartholomew had fed her and Luke well that morning, almost as a last meal. She hurried to Abbey's side and took her hand into her own.

Abbey looked at her with a mixture of relief and fear.

Mercy's heart twisted. There was no turning back. "Are you ready?"

"I don't know if I can do this," Abbey whispered.

"I'm here with you." But Mercy couldn't help the trepidation rising inside of her.

Abbey clutched Luke's hand tightly.

Two soldiers waited at the other end of the street, each wearing chainmail. One of the guards came forward.

Abbey pulled Luke closer to her. "No," Abbey whispered.

Mercy looked down at Luke. The boy's eyes snapped from the approaching soldier to his mother. Then he looked at Mercy before burying his face in the folds of his mother's skirt.

He clasped his mother's hand with both of his small ones.

"No," Abbey said, shaking her head. She held Luke's hand, refusing to give him up. "I said no! I won't give him up."

The guard stood for a long moment, looking at her. Then he took Luke's thin arm and began to pull him down the street to the bishop.

"You can't have him!" Abbey shouted, holding tightly to Luke's hand.

The guard ignored her and pulled until Luke's hand was torn from Abbey's.

"I said no! NOOO!" The wail echoed through the dirt streets of the village. Abbey stretched out her arms toward her young son.

None of the villagers gathered before the Wolf's Inn dared move. They shuffled uncomfortably and looked away from Abbey.

Mercy's heart pounded. Helplessness rose inside of her. The guard wasn't listening to Abbey. She glanced at Abbey's horrified expression and then back at the soldier.

The tall soldier in chainmail, with a sword strapped to his waist, held Luke's arm in a tight grasp. The child looked back at Abbey with tears streaming down his round cheeks. "Momma!"

"Noooo!" Abbey jerked forward toward the child. "You can't have him!"

The armored guard shoved the woman back with a firm hand as the child in his hold struggled to break free.

Mercy caught Abbey's shoulders, holding her back. She was afraid her friend would get hurt. "It will do no good, Abbey," she whispered quickly. "We'll get him back."

The words didn't console the frantic woman. She was desperate. She dodged out of Mercy's hold and ran to the child.

The men of the town stood, lining the street like statues, unable or unwilling to help.

The boy reached out his hands to his mother and Abbey

seized the child, drawing him against her to hold him protectively.

Mercy watched the horrible scene, her heart aching for her friend. It was inevitable that Abbey's son would be taken. They couldn't stop it. The soldier was hearing none of Abbey's cries. Luke would be taken. Mercy should have known that their plan wouldn't work. What did the guard care if the mother said no?

The guard reached for his weapon.

Horrified, Mercy hurried to Abbey's side, shouting at the guard to stop. She pressed her hand over his to prevent him from drawing his sword. "You can't! She is distraught! She is –"

"It is the law," the soldier snarled. "The bishop commands it." He shoved Mercy aside.

She fell on her back into the dirt of the road, the scene playing out in painful slow motion before her.

The guard ripped his sword free of its scabbard and lifted it high overhead. For a moment, it gleamed in the sunlight, reflecting a blinding blast into Mercy's eyes.

"No!" Mercy cried, reaching out to stop him.

Abbey lifted her arm to protect her child and herself against the sharp blow of the sword.

Nothing could stop the horrendous assault from happening. Nothing short of a miracle.

What happened was no miracle.

"Halt!"

The guard turned his head toward the stern voice, his arm still raised.

All eyes swiveled to the origin of the voice.

Clunk. Shuffle. Clunk. The golden rod hit the ground and the shuffling of the bright white robe against the dirt street sounded in the sudden silence. Over and over the sounds played as he came closer. Bishop Devdan.

Mercy couldn't help it. She hated him. She hated him with her entire being, but she was too fearful of him to say so out loud.

Abbey squeezed Luke to her, kissing the top of his head, mumbling, "Please. No."

Bishop Devdan pushed the guard's hand down and stepped past him to her side. "There is nothing to fear." He laid a hand on her bowed brown head.

Abbey squeezed her eyes closed; a strangled sob issued from her throat.

"It is the will of the Lord. As it was with Abraham. Do you fear the Lord?"

"He is my only child," Abbey whispered tearfully.

"God is testing you as he did Abraham. Whom do you love more? Whom do you fear more? What kind of destruction will the Lord level upon this village if you fail this test?"

For a moment, Abbey did not move. She stood as still as a rock.

Mercy climbed to her feet, wishing Abbey had the strength to deny him. Hoping that Abbey would not give up her son.

"Give him the boy, Abbey!" Simon shouted.

Mercy glanced up at Simon clutching his hoe before him as if he were ready to use it on Abbey. His brown eyes were narrowed, his lip raised in contempt.

Abbey squeezed her son, and slowly, slowly lowered her hands from him, staring him in the eye.

The bishop reached out and took the hand of the boy. The boy simpered, his eyes on his mother. "Come, child."

Abbey's shoulders slumped. She knelt before the bishop; her arms empty. Defeated.

Mercy stepped up to Abbey's side, drawing the gaze of the bishop. "Why would God do this? Why would he demand all our boys?"

The bishop looked at her, his dark eyes resting on her. His mouth quirked to the side. "Mercy, isn't it? I do not pretend to know the motives of the Lord." His eyes narrowed slightly.

A chill ran through Mercy.

"Perhaps in atonement for a sin. Perhaps to test you. Pray." He lifted his hands to the sky. "Pray, all of you! Pray for salvation."

Shivers shot through Mercy. Salvation. Eoos was her salvation. He was the answer to her prayers.

"Where is your beautiful boy?" the bishop asked Mercy.

Shocked, Mercy could not move. She was frozen to the spot.

"He is a beautiful child. I look forward to seeing him."

Mercy recoiled. How did he remember Kit?

He cast one last look at Mercy.

Her eyes narrowed, and her teeth clenched when his gaze touched hers. She quickly looked down at Abbey, placing an arm around her shoulders. When she looked up again, the bishop was walking away, Luke's hand in his.

Simon approached them. "Stupid woman," he grumbled. "You almost brought the wrath of God down upon us."

"You just stood there," Mercy whispered, helping Abbey to her feet.

"I'm not risking that. If my crops fail or there is a drought, that will be the end for all of us."

"I won't believe that God has demanded our children," Mercy stated, rubbing Abbey's arm. She cast a glance over her shoulder at the bishop. "This smells of humanity."

"You doubt the Bishop?" Simon demanded.

Mercy shook her head. She needed to bide her words. There were too many listening who would run to the bishop. "No. But I think we should stand together."

"We are!"

"You have no children. You don't know how it is to give one up. To make that kind of sacrifice."

"Your boy's the next sacrifice, isn't he? I'm not listening

to anything you say. You are just looking out for yourself and your child."

"I am going to pray for salvation," Mercy whispered. "Because it will not come from you."

She moved past Simon, supporting Abbey.

They had walked halfway down the road, away from the other villagers, when Abbey yanked herself free from Mercy's hold. "You just stood there. He took my son and you just stood there."

Mercy stared at Abbey in disbelief. "What could I have done?"

"Kill him," she snarled. "You promised. You promised me."

Shocked, Mercy opened her mouth, but nothing came out.

"Get away from me," she snarled.

"Abbey –" Mercy reached out to her.

"Go home."

Mercy stood numbly as Abbey stumbled past her. Her hands were still outstretched for her friend. Abbey was just upset, as she should be. But Mercy couldn't stop feeling guilty.

She turned and locked eyes with Eoos! He stood in the shadows just beside the baker's house with his horse. Frightened he would be discovered, she made her way to his side.

His stoic gaze was leveled down the street, on the path the bishop had taken. His jaw was clenched. "This shouldn't be allowed."

Sympathy and resolution washed over her. She took his arm and leaned her head against his shoulder as they walked back to the cottage, leading his horse.

"What does he do with the children?"

Mercy shook her head and shrugged. "No one knows. They are never seen again."

"Has anyone spoken to the bishop?"

"And said what?" She shook her head. "No. Everyone is afraid of him. He says this is punishment for our sins."

"What do you think?"

"I think I will do anything to save Kit. I won't let him go."

His gaze swept her. "How long has the bishop been taking the boys?"

She looked away at the rising moon, thinking back to the first time she arrived in Goodmont. "Since I married Dean. When I came into the town, it was already happening. I remember the first boy I saw the bishop take. I remember the mother was numb, almost as though she were drunk. She just let the bishop take her son. Her husband held her tightly in his embrace. The child was a beautiful boy with blonde hair and blue eyes, bright and always with a smile." She looked down. "I can't blame her really. She had other children. She couldn't deny the bishop."

"And the fathers? They don't fight? They don't protest?"

"Against the bishop? Against one of the church?" She half laughed. "No. They wouldn't dare. They've convinced themselves that the bishop needs the boys."

"Needs children?"

"Perhaps they are servants working for the church. Perhaps they..." But she couldn't think of anything a five-summers-old child could do that a grown man couldn't do better.

Silence spread for a moment until Eoos uttered the words, "Kit will be five soon."

Despair swept through Mercy and she felt a weight in her chest. She could only nod.

"What will you do?"

"I will find a strong knight to stop him," she whispered and lifted her gaze to lock with his. "I will ask him to help us. To save my son."

Chapter Seven

Eoos understood what she was asking. He stared down at her. He wanted to help; he had already promised Kit he would. But he was only one man. "What can I do against the bishop's men?"

Tears shimmered in her blue eyes. "There has to be some way. There must be something we can do. Won't you help us?"

"I can't even remember who I am. What would you have me do?"

"Please, Eoos."

His horse whinnied and tossed his head, bumping Mercy. She lost her balance.

Eoos quickly reached out and grabbed her arm to steady her. She regained her balance, and when he should have pulled his hand away, he didn't. She needed him. And she had helped him to heal, offering him food and a warm place to stay, seeing to his injuries. He was in-debted to her. He just didn't know what he could do. "I will do all I can."

She pulled her arm back until her fingers touched his and she squeezed his hand. "Thank you, Eoos."

The horse whinnied again.

Eoos cast the animal an annoyed glance and his gaze came to rest on their interlocked fingers. "Is there a magistrate you can speak to about this?"

Mercy shook her head. "I'm positive the bishop is paying him, or the magistrate doesn't believe us. He simply ignores the matter."

"Have you sent a missive to the Pope?" Mercy looked at him with such tenderness that his insides twisted.

"We don't know how to write."

"I do. We can start there."

"It will take weeks to get a missive to the Pope. Kit doesn't have weeks. I need to… to take him somewhere. Keep him hidden."

"You would leave? Run away?"

"I would do anything to keep Kit safe. But I have nowhere to go."

She was desperate. Her eyes were large with anguish, bright with agony. He brushed a lock of hair from her cheek.

"I'll write a missive. We'll start there."

Mercy nodded, but doubt furrowed her brow.

"If we hear nothing, we shall begin to plan an escape."

Mercy threw her hands around his neck, hugging him tightly.

Shocked, Eoos caught her and held her against him.

"I can't thank you enough," Mercy whispered.

Her body was soft, her cheek pressed against his even softer. Something stirred within him, something warm and comforting and needing. He wanted to protect her.

She pressed a kiss to his cheek before pulling back.

Startled, he could only stare at her. Her pert nose, her full lips. She smelled like the flowers and honey. When she stepped back, he immediately missed her warmth, her touch. He cleared his throat softly, the memory of her kiss still wet on his cheek.

Together, they walked down the dusty road toward the cottage. He turned to regard the village as it grew distant. It was a small village and the people were afraid. He wondered what he could do to help Kit. He would try everything.

"Did you remember anything about your horse?" Mercy asked.

Eoos looked at her, jarred out of his reverie. "No. Nothing." It was strange the way he recalled his past. He knew things, but he couldn't remember important things, like his name.

"You should ride him tomorrow."

Eoos nodded. A good suggestion. "Perhaps after I visit the inn."

"Do you remember how to ride?"

Eoos shrugged. "I'll try anything to remember."

They walked in silence, their footsteps crunching rocks and dirt.

"Is there anything you can tell me to help me remember?" He had a suspicion she knew more than she was telling him.

She was quiet for a long moment. "I didn't know you before the fight."

"You stopped it."

She nodded.

"What were you doing at the inn?"

"I wasn't at the inn when the fight started. Walter ran and told me."

"Why did you stop it?"

"I thought you were an answer to a prayer."

He gripped the reins for Pounder loosely but sternly. Maybe he was the answer to her prayer. He just didn't remember. "I must have done something bad for all the townsmen to beat me."

Mercy remained silent.

"I should talk to them."

"No!" Halting suddenly, she looked at him with wide, alarmed eyes. "I mean...then they would know you aren't my cousin. They would try to beat you again."

"Mercy," he said softly. "I have to find out who I am."

"You said you would help us."

"Aye. And I will. That won't change."

"I don't think speaking with the men who beat you is the answer. If they recognize you, all of our planning will be for naught. I don't want you hurt again."

"I have to find out. You must understand that."

She nodded, silent for a moment. Finally, she looked into the distance. "We'll go to the inn later this afternoon."

Elated, Eoos hoped to recover more of his memories.

Mercy knew she couldn't deny Eoos finding out the truth about who he was. It was cruel not to tell him. Misgivings plagued her. What if he wouldn't help them after he discovered he killed the Archbishop? It shouldn't matter. It shouldn't matter if he found out he had killed the Archbishop Thomas Becket. But something inside of her doubted him. What if he would not stop a man of the church? What if he decided that to save his soul, he should give Kit to the bishop? Or turn himself over to the bishop? Or what if the village men recognized him and killed him this time? That was why she had agreed to take him to the inn that afternoon. Most of the farmers would still be in the fields and Bartholomew would be at the baker getting grain and yeast to make ale.

When Alice arrived, Mercy went to search for Eoos. It wasn't hard to find him. When she called his name, Kit poked his head from behind the barn.

She hurried to him. He stood behind the barn, gazing at something. Eoos sat atop his horse, moving it back and forth across the field behind the barn. She joined Kit and watched him for a moment. There was never a more striking vision. His mastery of the horse was amazing. He sat tall in the saddle; a gentle breeze ruffled his dark hair.

"He's amazing," Kit whispered.

She had to agree.

Eoos spotted her and steered the animal toward them at an easy gallop. His face was healing, the swelling retreating. A large bruise still ringed his eye. The puffiness had receded from his lip. Even battered, she could still find beauty in his face. His hair ruffled by the breeze, his lips a sensual slash, the intense way he stared at her. Her insides liquified beneath his stare as heat engulfed her.

He stopped before them. "Good day, Mercy."

The tone in his voice sent ripples of excitement rushing through her. She ran a hand along the horse's neck. "Did you remember anything?"

"No," he admitted. "But I found that I knew how to saddle him."

She nodded. Yes. As a knight, he would know that. And as a knight, he would know how to command a horse.

"Are you ready to accompany me to the inn?"

His voice was a rich timbre that sent vibrations through her body. He knew how to command more than just a horse.

"We can ride there." He extended a hand to her.

She faltered.

"I want to go!" Kit called.

"This is work for adults," Eoos told Kit. "Your mother and I will return."

"Alice will have work for you," Mercy added.

"Awww," Kit grumbled, kicking a pebble.

Mercy lay a hand on Kit's head. Yes, Eoos knew how to command. Armies as well as children. She pressed a kiss to Kit's head. "We shan't be long."

Kit slowly moved toward the cottage, his head hung as he shuffled and kicked the dirt.

Mercy looked at Eoos. He extended his hand to her again. Mercy balked as tremors of delight ran up her spine.

Still, she resisted the temptation he offered. "I should saddle my mare."

"My horse is already saddled. A ride into the village will not over tax him."

Mercy glanced at the barn in hesitation. She didn't feel it appropriate to ride with him. So close. Together.

"What are you afraid of?" He pushed his hand at her.

That did it. She opened her mouth, then snapped it closed. She straightened her back and lifted her chin. "I'm not afraid." She placed her hand into his.

In one movement, he pulled her up before him. She squirmed as her hip hit the saddle.

He slid her over his legs more comfortably.

"This saddle isn't meant for two people," she complained softly.

He grinned, his lips quirking to the side; his eyes danced in merriment. "No, it's not." He spurred the horse.

She fell back against his strong, solid chest, having to hold onto the pommel of the saddle for balance. His arm slid around her waist, steadying her. She couldn't help but notice the comfort and ease with which her body molded to his. For a moment, she let herself imagine what it would be like to be held in his arms. Safe. Wanted. Desired. Oh, wicked, wicked thoughts. She had not felt or imagined these feelings since Dean had passed. Why now? When love should have been the farthest thing from her mind.

"The ride is not far?"

"No," she answered. "The inn is just up ahead and a little off the road." She pointed the way.

He guided the horse with ease, as if he had done it a thousand times before. "Still no memories?"

"No."

He followed her directions, and when the inn came into view, he reigned in his horse. The horse danced nervously, and he did not urge it on.

Mercy looked over her shoulder at him.

"It is as if there is something there, something I can't quite grasp but just out of my reach."

"How do you feel? Any headaches?"

He looked down at her with warm, grateful blue eyes.

"None." He swung his leg over the horse and dismounted, then reached up for her.

His hands spanned her waist and she placed her hands on his shoulders. Strong, amazingly muscled. She could feel rippling strength beneath her hands. For a moment, she stared at his face. Healing magnificently. The bruise around his eye was fading and his lips were almost back to normal except for the cut. Back to luscious, beckoning fullness. She mentally shook herself and stepped away from him.

He looked at the inn again and started toward it.

She trailed behind as he tied the horse to a nearby tree. She remembered the last time she had been here. She had rushed in to find him being beaten by five of the townsmen. He was laying on the floor, unconscious and bloodied. When she had first seen him, she didn't think he would survive.

He glanced at her. "You look as hesitant as I."

She shook her head, pushing the image from her mind. It disturbed her more than she was willing to admit.

The main room was dark and empty, except for a low fire in the hearth.

Eoos stepped past Mercy, scanning the room. His hand immediately went to his waist, where his scabbard would be. Tingles danced across the nape of his neck. An uneasy feeling filled him, and he suddenly wanted to rush from the inn. Instead, he stepped deeper into the room.

He looked at the fire and stopped before the flames. Warmth washed over him. He knew he had been here. This spot was familiar, like an old worn pair of boots, but his memories wouldn't come. He glanced over his shoulder at Mercy.

She stood with her hands clasped before her, staring at him with concern.

He grinned weakly, trying to comfort her. He knew she had not been at the attack until the end. And then, there came another image, one he had seen before. Mercy shouting, standing over him as she tried to push the other men back. She had stopped the attack.

Again, he looked at the fire. Another hot burst of pain erupted in his mind and he saw other flames. A torch, maybe. More shouting. Agony ripped through his mind. Shouting that echoed. He couldn't hear the words. A broken sword. *His* broken sword.

He felt hands on his shoulders, guiding him to a chair. He pressed his temples, wanting the agony to stop but needing to find out who he was, what had happened to his sword.

"Eoos!" Mercy called, worried.

Her voice came from far away. He opened his eyes to look into her large blue ones.

The door opened and a small girl emerged, wiping her hands on her brown cotton dress.

Images descended over Eoos like a rain. The girl speaking to him; a round bellied man shaking his head and waving his arms. "Outside!" the man cried. Blows rocked him. Again, and again they hit him. Pain with each strike. But he did not attack the men. He knew he could kill some of them with his fists, but he didn't.

"Eoos!" Mercy shouted, shaking him.

The agony filled his head until he wanted to cry out, until it blinded him and he could take no more. He clenched his teeth and willed the images away, but they would not be banished. He saw men standing over him, their fists descending again and again. He covered his head to protect it from the blows as well as the pain in his mind.

Something wet and cool pressed against his forehead. He opened his eyes to see Mercy wiping his brow with a damp wet cloth. The fire in his mind eased and the pain slowly faded. He looked at her worried stare. "I saw them," he gasped.

"Them?"

"Simon was one of them. But I couldn't see why they attacked me."

Mercy wiped the cool cloth down his cheek, over his jaw. "It doesn't matter. You must stop. This is too much. Too early. Wait until you recover more."

Eoos had to agree with her.

"Me da wants to know if he is going to pay," the small girl said timidly.

Eoos looked at her in confusion. "Pay? For what?"

"Your room at the inn."

Room. Eoos glanced up the stairs. More memories flooded through his mind until his head felt like it was being split open. Mercy was right. He needed to rest.

"Tell Bartholomew that I will pay," Mercy said. "Can you go and get some ale?"

The little girl bobbed her head and disappeared into a back room.

"Does she know who I am?" Eoos whispered, "My name?"

"Eoos," Mercy pleaded.

"Just a name. That will be enough for today."

Mercy sighed and nodded. "This is dangerous. You are in too much pain. As your head heals, the memories will come. You mustn't try to force them."

"What if they don't come?"

She stroked his cheek. Her hand was warm and tender and gentle and...loving. "They will."

Her words soothed him, and the pain slowly faded from his mind. He stood shakily and she steadied him with a hand on the back of his arm.

The child appeared from the back room holding a mug. She handed it to Eoos. He was about to raise the cup to his lips when he spotted the stairway leading up to another floor. He lowered the cup, a scowl on his brow. "I have a bag. Where is my bag?"

"It is back at my barn," Mercy said.

He looked at the little girl. "I procured a room for the night."

The girl simply stared at him.

"What is my name?"

"Me da says you are Sir Richard le Breton," she answered quietly. "The brute."

Chapter Eight

The brute. Richard mulled the word over on the ride back to the cottage. "Who is Eoos?" he finally asked as he helped Mercy dismount.

Mercy shrugged.

It was a name familiar to him. Comforting. But he didn't remember who it belonged to. Was he married? Did he have a family that was missing him?

Mercy walked toward the cottage.

Right now, his only family was Mercy and her boy, Kit. He had vowed to help them to save Kit.

"Mercy," he called.

She turned to him.

"I have given my vow to help you. But truth be told, we know nothing of my past. What if you are in more danger with me than you would be staying in this village?"

Mercy returned to him. She shook her head. "Kit is in more danger here. That is all that is important to me. They will not take him."

He nodded.

Mercy sighed softly. Her gaze swept his face in contemplation. "So, it's Richard now?" Mercy grinned. "I don't know if I'll get used to calling you that."

"It is my name."

She stared at him for a long moment. "Richard," she whispered. "Sir Richard." Finally, she nodded. "Yes. It fits."

"What about the brute?"

She scowled. "I would never call you that."

His heart warmed. "There must be a reason for others to call me that."

"Yes." She looked down, as if searching the ground for the answer. "Something from your past."

"I didn't remember my own name. What if I don't remember? What if it never comes back?"

"It will," she promised. "You've already started remembering. You knew how to ride."

"But I didn't recognize my horse."

"You knew how to clean armor and that you had a bag."

Richard grew silent. She was right. He just needed...to be patient. And he had a feeling that patience wasn't his strength. Perhaps that was where the name brute came from.

Kit burst from the cottage and raced across the yard toward them. There was something in his wide-eyed expression that sent ripples of trepidation down Richard's back.

Mercy held her arms out to him. "What is it?"

Kit leapt into her arms. "Simon is here."

The boy had no sooner gotten the words out when two men walked out of the cottage, Alice following. Mercy set Kit on his feet, pulling him behind her as Richard stepped forward protectively.

Richard recognized Simon, but the other he didn't know.

"You are not welcomed here," Mercy stated.

Richard summed up the second man with a sweeping glance. He had a round belly and scraggily shoulder length dark hair. Even injured, Richard knew the man posed no threat.

"I've brought Bartholomew. He can identify the brute," Simon snarled.

Mercy rose up. "He is not here. How many times must I tell you that?"

"We'll see. Stand aside and let Bartholomew look at...your cousin."

"How dare you come here to insult me. I told you the knight escaped. Are you calling me a liar?"

They were looking for him. To beat him again? "It's alright," Richard called from beside her. "Let him look."

Mercy glanced at him.

Richard saw uncertainty in her gaze. But he was not afraid. Nor was he a fool. He knew he was the knight they were looking for. He knew Mercy had cut his hair and dyed it. And he had shaved the thick beard from his chin. He hoped this would be enough to disguise his looks.

Bartholomew stepped up to him, his eyes narrowed. His gaze moved over his face.

Richard stared him in the eye.

Bartholomew's gaze moved down over his body.

Richard was grateful Mercy had given him a tunic from her late husband to wear. It was tight across his shoulders, and short, but it would do.

"Well?" Simon demanded.

Richard held his breath, preparing to defend himself with blows. They were foolish to confront him with no weapons for defense.

Bartholomew scratched his head. "I can't be sure."

"Is it him or not?" Simon demanded.

"I..." Bartholomew looked at Richard again. "No. It's not him."

His shoulders relaxed, draining of tension. "The lady has said you are not welcome here. Be gone. And never doubt her word again."

Simon grumbled. He whirled away, disappointed and angry.

Bartholomew joined him, and they both moved toward the road.

Richard looked at Mercy. Her face seemed pale in the afternoon sunlight.

They both watched the men move off down the road.

Richard chuckled. "I've never been so happy about shaving before."

Mercy looked at him, but there was concern in her gaze. "We still need to be careful. You're still healing. You can't defend yourself against everyone."

It irked him that she thought he was weak. That she thought he couldn't protect himself. He was a knight! He had slain and battled others! The thought sobered him. Had he killed?

"Besides. You are still recovering. I will be alright. Kit, bring Richard his bag. It's near my bed. I'm going to visit Abbey."

As Mercy drew closer to Abbey's cruck, she saw a crowd standing before the doorway, peering inside. Tremors of unease snaked down Mercy's spine. She hurried to the open doorway, having to push her way through the villagers.

Inside, Lief held Abbey around the waist. A rope around her neck pulled her upright, the other end tied to a rafter in the ceiling. Her cloudy eyes were open and stared at Mercy with condemnation. Her face was greyish blue.

Mercy gasped but couldn't look away.

Simon stood on a stool behind her and cut the rope tied to a rafter.

Mercy didn't have to examine Abbey. She knew she

was dead. She knew what had happened. She rushed into the room just as the rope broke and Abbey's body fell forward over Lief's shoulder. He caught her and moved to a nearby table.

Simon scurried down from the stool and cleared the table with a sweep of his arm.

Mercy jumped as a pottery jar crashed to the floor, shattering into pieces.

Lief reverently eased Abbey onto the table.

For a moment, Mercy couldn't move. Tears rose in her eyes as she stared at her friend. She couldn't help her. She should never have let her go home alone. She should have stayed with her.

She stepped up to Abbey's side. There was nothing she could do for Abbey now. She was gone.

Mercy reached out and brushed her hand over Abbey's eyes, easing them closed. She bid her a silent farewell as heavy guilt settled over her shoulders. She never should have left her.

"She killed herself," Lief whispered in disbelief.

"What a weak woman," Simon grumbled.

Mercy whirled on him. "How dare you disrespect her like that? You were too cowardly to stand up for her child. Her death is on your shoulders." She stepped away from Simon. "It's on all our shoulders." She glanced back at Abbey's body. "The bishop took her life. There was nothing left for her." Fear tightened a lump in her chest as tears rushed through her eyes. She pictured her face over Abbey's. Would she do the same thing if the bishop took Kit?

No. There had to be a way. Some way to save Kit. And herself. She had been unable to save Luke, how was she going to save Kit?

Richard sat on a straw bale in a circle of flickering candlelight. He pulled open a flap on his bag. Kit had brought him his bag, the one they had brought from the inn. He had to know who he was. He had to remember his past. Maybe something inside the bag could help him remember. He shoved his hand inside the cotton bag. He pulled out clothing. A tunic, a pair of leggings. Nothing he remembered. He plunged his hand inside again and pulled out a knife sharpening rock. A knight would have that. He was surprised he remembered what it was. He reached inside and pushed his hand back and forth. His fingers wrapped around something metallic, round and small at the bottom of the bag. He brought it forth. Coins. He tossed them aside, aggravated. They lent nothing to who he was.

Frustrated, he took the bag and turned it over, dumping the contents onto the dirt floor. More coins rolled across the dirt, clothing and rags fell out. He spread the contents on the ground, searching. Nothing. Nothing that helped him remember.

He stood and ran his hands through his hair, pushing it from his face. The moonlight shone in through the slats of the barn wall. He had to know. There was something everyone was hiding from him. What had he done? What had happened? He gritted his teeth and paced. There had to be something! He kicked the bag and it flew across the stall, hitting the far wooden wall with a dull clunk.

Surprised and confused, Richard turned to eye the bag. It should have been empty. It should have made no sound.

He approached the bag slowly and stood over it for a long moment. His shadow covered the burlap sack completely. He bent down and reached for it, weighing it in his hand. It felt empty. But wait... There was something... He crumbled the bag in his hand until he felt something hard wedged inside. He held the bag so as not to lose the item within. It was strange. It seemed to be hidden within the sack, but there were no pockets that he could find to shelter the item. He turned the sack, but there was no way to get to it. Frustrated, he paused, a fierce scowl on his brow. He glanced around the stall, searching for something to aid him. Leaning against the wall of the barn, Richard spied a scythe. He attached part of the sack to the sharp metal blade and pulled. The bag ripped and something fell to the ground. He bent to pick the item up.

A small golden cross. He turned it over. Tingles danced across the nape of his neck. It was bejeweled with rare and sparkling gems. Expensive. No wonder he had hidden it.

"Richard?"

At Mercy's voice, he spun to find her rushing into the barn. He instinctively tucked the cross into the waist of his leggings. "I'm here." He moved to greet her.

She hurried to him.

At her anguished look, Richard asked, "What is it?"

For a moment, she said nothing. Her desperate gaze swept his face.

He touched her arm, trying to soothe her. "Did something happen?"

Tears sparkled in her eyes. "Abbey is dead."

Richard frowned, his gaze moving over Mercy's distraught expression. "What happened?"

"Luke was everything to her," Mercy gasped. "She… She took her own life."

Richard led her to a bale of hay and had her take a seat on it. "I'm sorry."

"I hate this. Watching as the bishop and his guards come down the road to take a child. The villagers come out to watch but do nothing. They stand by and let him take the boys." Her fingers curled to fists on the straw.

"I've written the letter to the Pope and had Kit take it into town." He could tell by her slumped shoulders and clutched hands that it wasn't enough. "I can object, at your side, to the bishop taking Kit."

"Abbey objected. She told them no, that they couldn't have Luke. It did no good."

"I am a knight. My duty is to protect the innocent." He straightened his shoulders. "I will fight them."

Gratitude shone from her shimmering eyes. "They might throw you in the dungeon for heresy or you might die. That's not the answer. We have to stop the bishop. He needs to..." She looked at him intensely. "Die."

Richard balked. "Mercy. Don't say that. He is a man of the cloth. He is defenseless."

"So are the children." She shook her head. "I'm sorry. I just... I hate him! He should be good and kind, but he is compassionless and cold." She stood and paced before him. "What kind of man takes children to work in the name of God?"

"Children are assigned to lords as pages at a young age. Perhaps there is nothing to fear."

Mercy searched the ground with her eyes as if the answer were there. "Pages are given up willingly. This feels wrong. I can't explain it." She sat beside him, taking his hands into hers. "I'm afraid."

Richard pulled her into his embrace, holding her tightly. He felt her body shake with a suppressed sob. He wanted to comfort her. All he could think of doing was holding her close. She was warm and soft. She pressed her face against the hollow of his shoulder as he stroked her hair. "I won't let them take Kit."

She pulled back to look up at him. So vulnerable. So desperate.

His gaze moved over her face. Beautiful. Soft. Tempting. He pushed a strand of hair from her cheek. Her lips were so full and tempting. And then she was leaning in. Instinctively, he cupped the back of her head and pulled her to him. Longing speared through him at the touch of her lips. His mouth moved over hers gently in reassurance. As the flames of passion ignited within him, the kiss deepened.

He urged her lips to part and she willingly obliged. He thrust his tongue forward, tasting her, exploring every luscious corner of her mouth.

She answered by pulling him tightly against her; her tongue meeting and battling his.

Lord, how he wanted her. All of her. Beneath him. He wanted to touch and savor every inch of her delectable body. But not now. Breathing hard, he pulled away, separating from her. In her lidded eyes, he saw need and desire. His own need hardened in his leggings. Damn, he wanted her.

He didn't think it right to take her without knowing his past. Without knowing if he was committed to someone else. "Mercy…"

She grinned and ducked her head. "It's alright. You're a knight and I'm –"

"No." He caught her chin and lifted it. "I have to find out who I am before I can give myself to you. Before I can make you mine."

Her gaze moved over his face, touching him with understanding. She bobbed a nod.

"Make no mistake, my fiery wench, I will have you in the beat of a heart if I am able." She smiled at that. "Do you understand?"

"Yes," she answered and rose. "I shall wait for you to find yourself."

Richard nodded. Everything in him wanted to save her. To save her son. "Until I do, pack. We will leave immediately. Get as far away from Goodmont as we can."

"Leave?" She looked around.

"Perhaps when Kit is older, we can return. But this is truly the only way to escape the bishop."

She nodded with excitement. Her eyes held hope. "I'll start packing."

Richard watched her leave. His heart was filled with tenderness and possibility. He was doing the right thing.

He had one thing he needed to do first. She wouldn't even know he was gone. His hand closed around the cross tucked into his waistband.

Chapter Nine

Richard ducked back behind a bush, watching the cathedral. He reached down and adjusted the cross in his waistband. The golden cross, embedded with gems. He had thought it was rare, until he saw the exact same cross hanging from the bishop's neck. A smaller version, but exactly the same. The fact that the bishop had the same cross as he did sent shivers across his neck. It couldn't be a good sign. But that was not why he had come. He came to watch and see if he could find any of the boys.

He looked up at a cross high above the angled rooftop. A shadow against the gray night sky. A beacon.

Pain burned the back of his mind. Why would his head hurt if this wasn't related to his past? His fingers wrapped tightly around the concealed cross. The throbbing in his mind became the beat of a drum. He glanced up at the tall spire above his head, at the cross there. Suddenly, a blinding flash of white pain overcame him, and he saw another cross. He heard distant shouting. He saw blood against a white cloth. A broken sword.

He doubled over, holding his head.

In his mind, his fingers were wrapped around the hilt

of the sword! The broken sword.

The door of the cathedral opened, and the bishop stepped out.

Richard was wracked with pain. He watched through a white haze of agony as horses were brought out for the bishop and the three guards that followed him. He winced, squeezing his eyes to slits. The bishop and guards mounted the horses. And then, Simon walked out of the cathedral.

Shock filled Richard. He glanced back down the road toward Goodmont. Mercy! He stumbled toward his horse, but a blinding flash of lightning pierced his mind with such agony that he leaned against the horse for support and could go no further. He groaned, pressing his fingers against his eyes. A broken sword. Blood. Blood against the white robe. The cross he held lying in the blood. The red liquid surrounded it in a frame.

Such anguish ripped through his mind that he fell to his knees. But the memories wouldn't stop. He remembered. He remembered it all.

He was a murderer.

Oh, he hated him. Archbishop Thomas Becket was the reason his friend William could not marry the woman he loved. They had been connected by kinship relationship somewhere far down the line. She was a double second cousin of William, but Becket had not granted the couple a dispensation from affinity so they could marry in the church. William had died of a broken heart shortly after. It was all Becket's fault!

As Richard and his friends, William de Tracy, Reginald FitzUrse, and Hugh de Morville marched up to Canterbury cathedral, that was all he could think of. His dead friend, William. That and they were following the king's order to rid him of the priest.

After two monks opened the door to the cloister, Reginald shouldered his way in, and the knights followed.

Long wooden tables lined the hall, each filled with monks who had stopped eating to stare at the knights.

"Where is Thomas Becket?" Reginald demanded.

Not one of the monks said a word.

Richard stepped forward. "Where is the traitor?" he growled.

"We bear a message from King Henry!" Reginald added. "Speak up!"

Richard grimaced. The only message he knew of was a command from King Henry to rid him of this troublesome priest.

Finally, a man dressed in white robes stood from one of the tables. He lifted his chin. He had the confidence of leadership about him. "I am here, FitzUrse," Archbishop Thomas Becket said. "Why do you disturb these monks at mealtime?"

"By the king's orders, you are to return with us to England," Reginald commanded.

"I do not answer to the king, but to One in higher authority. I will not return to England."

The impudence! Richard snarled. Treason! Who did he think he was? He had heard of Becket's attitude but thought surely he would make the right choice when faced with four armed knights.

"You defy the king?" William asked, shocked.

"I answer only to one rule. His rule."

Reginald stepped forward. "All who are on the side of the king, hinder the archbishop! Do not let him leave!" He whirled and stormed from the hall.

Richard moved quickly after him. "We're not leaving."

"No."

As they moved out of the cloister, the monks began to whisper amongst themselves. Richard knew they would not stand against Becket. Some monks even rose and gathered near the archbishop in fear and protection, searching for guidance and direction.

Impudent servants, Richard thought with disdain.

"The monks will protect him. We don't have a choice," Reginald said as he put on his armor.

Richard gladly agreed. He needed no convincing.

"They are defenseless!" Hugh exclaimed. "What kind of knights are we if we cannot overpower a man of the cloth?"

"There are many of them and only four of us," Richard said.

He strapped on his sword. "We will use whatever force we must to take the archbishop to King Henry."

"Aye!" Reginald agreed.

William put a hand on Reginald's arm. "No harm will come to Becket."

William had always been the softest of the group. It didn't surprise Richard that he didn't want to harm Becket.

Reginald jerked his arm free of William's hold. "We will take him by force, if need be. But he will return to Henry." He held out his hand to William. "Are you with us?"

Richard wouldn't have been surprised if William had left. But they were friends. They had all come this far. They had all agreed this was what King Henry had ordered.

Finally, William nodded and clasped Reginald's arm. "With you."

Reginald grinned. Richard nodded in agreement.

"Quickly, sirs!" A monk raced out of the doors of the cloister toward them. His cold breath formed a puff with each breath he took. He pushed his hood from his head. "He has escaped into the cathedral! This way!"

He was not going to escape. He had caused so much trouble for King Henry. Becket would not escape, Richard vowed. They would bring him to England alive or dead.

The four knights quickly finished putting on their armor and followed the monk toward Canterbury Cathedral. The wooden doors were closing as they approached, and the monk came up short, stopping on the stairs to the cathedral.

Richard rushed by the monk and launched himself against the door, as did the rest of the knights. They pushed against the doors to prevent them from closing and locking. At first, there was resistance. Richard shoved harder, using his anger against Becket to fuel his strength.

Suddenly, the doors swung open. As they entered, a group of monks fled to the side wall. They had been trying to keep the doors shut to prevent them from entering.

"King's men!" Reginald shouted, his voice echoing through the large vaulted room.

Near the altar, monks gathered together in fear. Even more brown robed monks clustered together in groups along the walls. Richard stormed toward the altar, following Reginald.

"Where is Thomas Becket, traitor to the king?" Reginald demanded.

The monks remained silent, fearful. Terrified. They clung together.

The knights walked down the aisle, past statues of saints and angels. Two large white pillars stood at either side of the altar.

Richard's gaze scanned the cathedral for Becket. He would bring the archbishop back to face the King. He would make sure Becket answered for his insolence.

"Where is the archbishop?" Reginald demanded.

Becket emerged from behind a group of monks, easing them gently aside as if parting a curtain. "Here I am, ready to suffer in the name of He who redeemed me with His blood. God forbid that I should flee on account of your swords or that I should depart from righteousness."

Richard growled softly. "Absolve and restore to communion those you have excommunicated and return to office those who have been suspended!" Becket had excommunicated bishops who took the king's side. All were innocents who failed to follow Becket's command. He used his power to punish them.

Murmurings grew louder near the door they had entered through, where monks had gathered. Hugh quickly raced to them, brandishing his sword before them to discourage any interference.

The archbishop shook his head, lifting his chin. "No penance has been made, so I will not absolve them."

He was speaking specifically of the Bishops of London and Salisbury who had supported the king. In revenge, the archbishop excommunicated them. Enraged at his insolence, Richard pulled his sword from its sheath. He would teach him not to defy the king!

"If you do not do as the king commands, then you will die," Reginald threatened.

The archbishop stood his ground, refusing to obey Reginald's command to come forth and allow himself to be taken to the king.

Richard's hand tightened around the hilt of his sword. So be it.

As one, the three knights lurched forward. William's hand grasped hold of the archbishop's white garments, attempting to drag him from the altar.

Reginald also grabbed the Archbishop's arm, pulling him, trying to force him from the altar.

The archbishop seized hold of one of the pillars, holding tight. He fought back, shoving Reginald away from him. "Don't touch me, FitzUrse! You owe me fealty and obedience, you who foolishly follow your accomplices."

Reginald stumbled, but quickly righted himself. He raised his sword. "I don't owe fealty or obedience to you who are in opposition to the fealty I owe my lord king."

One of the monks threw himself protectively before Becket.

William pulled at Becket's robes, trying to free him from the pillar which he clung to.

Cries and murmurings came from the monks at the rear of the cathedral where Sir Hugh was holding them back.

Richard grabbed the monk who was protecting Becket and twisted his arms, trying to disengage him from the archbishop.

As chaos ensued, Becket inclined his head. "I commend my cause and that of the Church to God, to St. Mary and to the blessed martyr, Denys."

With a cry of frustration, Reginald brought his sword down. The monk hugging the archbishop for protection lifted his arm to stop the blow. The sword hissed through the air, cutting the monk's raised arm and landing on the archbishop's head. The monk screamed in pain. Clutching his arm, he staggered away.

Blood trailed down the side of Becket's face.

Now perhaps Richard thought the archbishop would realize they meant to take him to the king.

William lifted his sword and brought the flat part down upon Becket's head. It landed with a dull thud.

Remarkably, the Archbishop still stood and stumbled from the pillar.

Reginald shoved the archbishop and he fell to his knees and elbows.

With a sick realization, Richard knew he would never go to the king, never follow the king's orders. Disgusted at his impudence, Richard lifted his sword high in the air. His teeth clenched tightly. "Take that for the love of my lord William!" He brought the weapon down as hard as he could, using all his strength. The sword hit with such fury that it cut deeply into Becket's head, slicing through his skull to land on the stones below. The sword hit the floor with a loud clang, jarring Richard's arms, and the metal blade split in two.

The archbishop collapsed and his blood flowed over the stones and down the steps.

Richard remembered everything. With his memories came a heavy cloak of guilt.

Mercy emerged from the cottage, almost bouncing. She was so full of excitement and joy. Richard had granted her hope. Salvation. The moon was high overhead and a wind whipped around her as she approached the barn. They were leaving. She was almost done packing. Just the food and…
She noticed that Richard's horse was not there. Confused, she swept into the barn, searching for Richard. But he was not there.

Scowling, she called, "Richard!" The darkness was complete. Everything was silent except for the creaking of the barn in the wind. "Richard!" she called desperately. Where was he? A rippling of trepidation snaked across her shoulders. She turned the corner to his stall, but it was empty. Where had he gone?

Confusion filled her. Where was he?

His horse was gone. Had he left? She quickly pushed the thought aside. For a moment, a fog clouded her mind. Why would he leave? Perhaps he went somewhere. Back to the inn? Why? Why would he do that? She was just making excuses.

Had he remembered who he was?

The thought sent a paralyzing fear through her. She should have told him. She should have told him the entire truth. That he was one of the knights who killed Archbishop Thomas Becket. But she was afraid he would leave her. And she needed him. Desperately.

Quickly, she pushed all the thoughts aside. It didn't matter. The only thing that mattered was Kit. Still, Richard had promised to help her, to save Kit.

Again, she shoved the thoughts aside. Even if he had left, it made no difference. She had to concentrate on saving Kit. There was only one thing she could do. Continue with the plan. Leave Goodmont. She rushed back across the yard and into the cottage. Finish packing.

Mercy's mind churned. What was left? Food. She quickly took a blanket from her bed and tied all four corners together. She began to place some of the leftover bread into the make-shift bag. Food. Ale. She searched beside her bed. She knew she had a flask somewhere.

"Mercy?"

She whirled.

Walter stood in the doorway. He glanced at Kit's sleeping form before moving to her. "What are you doing?" he whispered.

Relief swept through her. "Help me. I'm packing." She continued searching for the flask. "I can't stay here."

"You're leaving?" he asked with exasperation.

Mercy searched beneath the straw. Her hand closed around something leather and she brought it forth with a sigh. Dean had won this in a dice game before she knew him. They had never used it.

Walter walked up to her. "Think about what you're doing. You can't just leave in the middle of the night!"

She shot to her feet. "I have to! Look what happened to Abbey! I'm not going to end up like that. I'm not going to let them have Kit!" She moved around Walter to the blanket, tossing the flask into it.

"You have time. You don't have to go right now."

"What difference will it make if I leave now or later? Will Simon or Lief or Roger or any of them change their mind and help me? Will the bishop let me keep Kit?" Her voice broke on the last. "I won't end up like Abbey."

Walter sighed softly. "Where is your knight?"

Despondence settled across Mercy's shoulders. "I don't know. He's gone. His horse is not here."

"He left?"

"I don't know."

"I told you to turn him over to the bishop."

Mercy shook her head. "It wouldn't have mattered. The bishop would still want Kit."

"It's dangerous on the road at night. At least wait until sunup."

Mercy felt impending doom all around her. Richard was gone. She was alone. She glanced at Kit. He was all she had. Her heart swelled inside her. How could she protect him?

"Think of your boy, Mercy. Think of the danger you will face alone on the road. Wait until sunup."

With a sigh, she nodded in agreement. It would give Richard time to return from wherever he went. It would give her time for her final hope. "Only until sun up."

Despite Mercy's best efforts, she continually looked for Richard. She had come to depend on him more than she realized. They had planned to escape together. She ran her fingers over her lips.

She had trusted him.

Her insides twisted tight. She glanced one last time at

the road as the sun began to rise, hoping and wishing to see his strong form riding toward her. But the dirt road remained empty and quiet. Disappointment crested inside of her. She returned to the cottage. She had already loaded the horse, and there was just one more thing to do. She gathered Kit into her arms. He stirred, but she kissed his forehead, whispering, "Quiet, Kit. Sleep, little one."

She ducked beneath the curtain and stepped outside…
…and froze. Standing on the road, as if waiting for her, were Simon, Thomas and Bartholomew. What made her gasp was the three soldiers and Bishop Devdan that were also there on horses. Her mouth dropped and she clutched Kit to her. She glanced at her horse, but she knew she could never outrun them. She straightened her back. "Bishop Devdan," she greeted. She shot a condemning glare to Simon.

"My dear," the bishop said. He slowly dismounted and held his hand out. One of the soldiers dismounted and placed his golden cane in his hand. Clunk. Shuffle. Clunk. He approached her.

Mercy squeezed Kit tightly, protectively. "It is not time."

"No," the bishop agreed. "But I have been told that you intend to flee." He glanced at her horse and back to her.

"Flee?" her voice quivered. "No! I am going to visit my cousin. One of them is ill and –"

The bishop cocked his head. The round purple zucchetto covering part of his balding head tilted with the movement. "I've heard enough of your lies, child."

She held Kit firmly against her, panic clawing inside of her. "Who told you I was lying? Simon? He just doesn't believe me! Bart?"

Bishop Devdan swiveled his head to the men.

Mercy followed his stare. Simon stepped aside and Walter moved forward. A whispered gasp escaped Mercy's lips and her chest tightened with betrayal.

"It's for the village, Mercy," he whispered.

"He told me everything," the bishop said. "He told me your plans to take your beautiful boy and run away and deny the Lord's orders."

Mercy shook her head as tears welled in her eyes.

Kit opened tired eyes and turned his head.

"He told me you lied to the village men in order to conceal a criminal."

The betrayal ran even deeper and again Mercy shook her head. She looked at Walter, but he would not meet her stare.

"He told me you protected a man who killed Archbishop Becket."

Simon's lip twisted in contempt.

"He told me that you wanted him to kill me."

Treachery sliced through her, but even more so, desperation. The bishop knew everything! Mercy could do nothing but deny the allegations. She glanced at the guards and shook her head fiercely. "No," she whispered in denial.

"Another lie?"

"No. No! It's not a lie. I would never want to kill. It's a sin," she stated emphatically. "It's a sin."

"Hmmm," the bishop mused. "It seems to me this village is in need of much redemption." His gaze dropped to Kit. He reached an old, wrinkled hand out to the boy.

Instinctively, Mercy pulled him away from the bishop's tainted touch.

The bishop's dark gaze snapped to hers.

For just a moment, Mercy saw fierce anger burning in his orbs. Then, it was gone.

He seemed to weigh the situation for a moment, staring down thoughtfully at the boy. "I need to have something so I know you are truly repentant." His lips twisted. "Give me the knight."

Mercy's heart dropped. Desolation swept through her as she realized there was no escape for her or for Kit. She knew Abbey's desperation. "I don't know where he is."

The bishop leaned in. "A shame."

She realized he had known this already. It was all a plan to get Kit. She placed Kit's feet on the ground, eyeing the soldiers. "It's not time," she whispered. "You need to show me that you are truly sorry for the sins you've committed."

Mercy's trembling hand tightened around Kit's arm. They were here to take him from her, to punish her. She remembered Abbey's soul-wrenching cry when they took Luke. Desperate, she knelt and embraced Kit. She held him tightly, tears entering her eyes. She would do anything, *anything* to save him. "I love you," she whispered, and pressed a kiss to his head. Her heart pounded with anguish. "Run," she whispered to him. Then, she pulled back and gently but urgently shoved him toward the forest. "Run!"

For a moment, nothing happened. Then, Kit dashed toward the forest.

"Stop him!" the bishop commanded.

Mercy ran after Kit, but only to interfere with the soldiers' pursuit. She stepped in front of them, following Kit and purposely slowed her run, giving Kit time to enter the forest. One of the soldiers shoved her aside. She fell to her knees, scrapping her knee and palm on the ground. She watched them from her hands and knees as they disappeared into the forest after Kit in the rising sunlight.

"Run," she whispered, half to Kit, half in prayer.

Clunk. Shuffle. Clunk. The sound stopped directly behind her. Tremors moved through her.

"You have not been penitent."

She was so glad. At least he would never have Kit.

"You are not sorry for your sins." There was a tight anger in the bishop's voice.

Mercy was not listening to him. She was listening to the shouts from the forest.

"This way!"

"Over here!"

Then, Kit's cry. "Let go!"

"Aw! Ya little brat!"

"Run," she whispered again.

"I know where he was going," the bishop stated.

Anguished terror snaked through her. She swiveled her head to look at the bishop. He stood in the rising sun cast in a red glow, shadows playing over his face. He looked inhuman. The bishop turned his head toward the group of villagers.

"As I said," he continued, "he told me everything."

Mercy's gaze settled on Walter. Agony sliced through her like a blade. Walter knew everything. She had trusted him completely, confided in him. She tried to rise, but the bishop put a hand on her shoulder and shoved her back to the ground with surprising strength.

"Stop it!"

At Kit's cry, Mercy's hands curled in the dirt in desperation.

They emerged from the forest. One soldier held Kit's arm tightly. The other two soldiers walked behind them, crashing through the brush.

Mercy began to shake. The forest blurred against the onslaught of tears rushing through her eyes. She wouldn't give up. She whirled on the bishop. "What do you want him for? He doesn't want to go!"

"We don't always get what we want or what is good for us."

"Take me instead! He's just a boy!"

"You?" His gaze moved over her in repulsion. "You are flawed. You are a sinner. The boy is innocent yet. I can mold him into a man worthy to work for God."

Kit pulled against the soldier's hold. "Mom!"

"Keep fighting, Kit. Don't stop. Don't stop."

"Can't you see that I am doing what is best for the boy?" the bishop asked.

"You don't know him! You don't know what is best for him. Let him go!" With an angry growl, Mercy pulled the dagger from her belt and lunged at the soldiers like a cat. The first soldier, the one holding Kit, sidestepped her attack. As she turned with the dagger raised, the second soldier caught her arm and twisted it savagely until pain wrenched her elbow. She dropped the dagger.

"You were going to run away with him and put the rest of the village in danger. Who were you thinking of? Yourself." The bishop turned and walked toward his horse.

"Mom!" Kit cried as he was dragged toward the horses.

Mercy rushed to follow, but the second soldier grabbed her around the waist, restraining her. She twisted and turned to break free, but the soldier's hold was not gentle nor was it weak. He held her firmly.

The bishop turned as Kit neared. "You shall be my greatest accomplishment," he whispered.

Kit kicked the bishop in the shin.

The bishop's pale face turned red, but he did not double over. "Bind him," he said through clenched teeth.

"No!" Mercy struggled. She whirled, clenching her fist, and hit the soldier holding her in the nose. Startled, hurt, he released her, and she dashed forward across the clearing toward her son.

Simon stepped in front of her, grabbing her arm. "Let him have the boy."

She shoved him away from her, hard, and continued.

Just before the horses, just as they put Kit on the horse, she was stopped. Walter grabbed her arm.

"The village will thrive. It's best for us all," Walter said.

"Best for you," she growled. She pushed at Walter's hold. Then Simon and Bartholomew were there, restraining her. Holding her back from reaching her son.

"They'll kill you," Walter said.

"No," she pleaded.

The soldier she had hit mounted his horse, holding his

nose.

The bishop cast one last look at her, a cold stare, before he urged his steed down the road.

Mercy pushed and twisted against the arms that held her as the horses moved down the road, as her boy moved farther and farther from her. A guttural cry welled up inside of her. No. They couldn't have taken him. This can't be happening.

When the bishop's horses were finally out of sight, the village men released her. She jerked forward, but they were gone. Kit was gone. Her entire body shook.

Simon and Bartholomew stepped by her, moving down the road back to their homes.

"This is for the best, Mercy. You must see that," Walter whispered.

She whirled on him, glaring hatred and fury. She saw nothing except betrayal, desolation.

"It's for the best." With a sigh, even Walter left her.

The sun rose behind her and she could do nothing but stand there watching the empty road. They were gone. Kit was gone. Mercy stood for a long time, staring. Waiting for Kit to come running back.

The worst pain she had ever felt pierced her chest. She felt lost in a fog of despondence and dropped to her knees as tears rushed to her eyes. She couldn't protect him. She had failed.

"You knew who I was."

Even his voice could not alleviate the despair. Richard. She had put all of her hope in him for nothing. He had not been there when she needed him most. Now, nothing mattered.

"You wanted me to kill the bishop because of what I had already done. Because I had already killed Becket."

Nothing mattered. "Where were you?" she whispered.

"You used me! Or you planned to. You didn't care about me. You only wanted me to kill the bishop."

She turned to him. A shadow against the rising red sun. "Why didn't you help me? Why didn't you help Kit?" "Help you?" he echoed, shocked. It didn't matter. In the end, no one had helped her. Her shoulders slouched and she turned away from him to look at the dusty ground. A small footprint no bigger than her hand was outlined by the dirt of the road. Kit's footprint. She ran a finger along the outline. She hadn't been able to protect him. Her defeat was total. They had her boy. What could she do? And then, she thought of Abbey. Her friend. Abbey couldn't live with the fact that they had taken her son.

"Where's Kit?"

A numbing death washed over her. "They took him." How could she live without Kit? She stood on shaky legs and stumbled back to the cottage. The bag she had packed for her escape lay open on the ground; the bread loaves had tumbled out into the dust. She moved the curtain aside and stepped into the cottage. Everywhere she looked, she saw Kit. His straw mattress. The table he ate at. The chickens he chased. She gasped a ragged sigh. She collapsed on his straw mattress, clutching her stomach. What was she to do? What was she to do?

And then her gaze lighted on a piece of rope used to corral the chickens. She reached out to it. Abbey had known her anguish. She clutched the rope in her hand. Abbey had given up her life as well as her boy. Because Luke was her life. Just as Kit was hers.

"What are you doing?"

Chapter Ten

"What are you doing?" Richard stared at Mercy. He didn't like the anguish on her face, he didn't like the way she was looking at that damned rope. It shouldn't matter! *She* shouldn't matter! Yet, guilt ate away inside him. He should have been there to help her. But how? He had no weapon, no sword. And yet, he knew if he was there, he would have fought to save Kit.

He couldn't take his eyes from her. Sitting slumped over on Kit's bed, that rope held loosely in her small hands. He took a step into the cottage. "What are you doing?"

"I would have killed him," she whispered. "To save Kit, I would have killed the bishop." She lifted such tormented eyes to him that Richard was taken aback. An immediate need to help her filled him. "This is what hell is. I'm already there."

Richard grimaced. She knew nothing of hell. Or perhaps she did. Now. They called him the Brute. Compassionless. Yet, he felt the desire to go to her and gather her in his arms.

"There is no life without him," she whispered, looking down at the rope. "Abbey knew this."

Richard didn't like her hopelessness. He didn't like the way she was looking at the rope. He crossed the room in two large strides and stood before her, his arms crossed. "What are you going to do?"

Mercy shook her head. Her eyes filled with tears. She stared down at the rope for a long moment. "Anything," she finally whispered.

"Anything?" he demanded. He towered over her. She had lied to him, kept his identity a secret. He owed her nothing. Except... he recognized the desolation in her eyes. She was alone. A loneliness he lived with every day. And the boy. The child was innocent. And truthfully, he had enjoyed the child's company. He was strong and clever. He couldn't let the bishop have him.

She threw the rope across the room. "Anything I can to get Kit back."

His eyes narrowed. That was the Mercy he knew. He nodded once. "I'll find the children."

She looked up at him, staring blankly as if she didn't understand his words. "How will you find him when no one could find the other children?"

"Is that what they told you? And you believe them? Someone somewhere knows where they are. I'll bring Kit back." He turned and started toward the doorway.

"Why?"

Richard grunted. "Because I am a fool." He walked to the curtain that sheltered the cottage from the outside world, and paused. He cast a glance back at her. "You are to wait here. Do you hear me?"

Her expression melted and she stared at him with such wonder that he became uncomfortable.

"I'm not doing this for you," he said firmly. "I'm doing this for the boy."

She stood.

For the first time, Richard realized how fragile she was. How slim and tiny. How utterly brave to be the common sense of the village.

"We should go after the bishop now. Follow them."

Disbelief filled him. "I have no sword. What would you have me do against armed men?" Hardness filled him at her betrayal. "Unless you are still planning to trade me for Kit."

"I'm going with you."

"Hear you nothing that I say, woman?" he demanded as she crossed the room toward him.

"The village men will try to stop you if they know what you are planning."

"All the more reason for you to stay and keep my secret."

She shook her head. "They don't know where you are. They think you've gone. You can't trust any of them. *I* can't trust any of them." She shook her head firmly, a lock of dark hair swung free from her braid. "I can't stay here. I don't want to."

"It's not your decision." Richard left the cottage and walked to the barn.

"I want nothing further to do with Goodmont."

At least there was a blush in her cheeks and purpose in her eyes. "You are not coming with me. You will only slow me down."

"Then I will look for Kit myself." She whirled and headed toward her horse.

"God's blood!" Richard stormed after her. He grabbed her arm and spun her around. "They know you! You can't just walk into the cathedral and start searching for Kit."

She lifted her chin. "How will you do it?"

"Oh, no!" He wiggled a finger before her face. "I'm not giving you that information so you can use it."

"Richard, please. I can help you. There's nothing for me here now. My entire life is with that evil man."

His eyebrows rose. "The bishop?"

"Not all men of the cloth are holy."

Tingles danced along the nape of his neck. That is what

he had thought of Archbishop Thomas Becket, the man he had killed. And it had gotten him into a whole world of trouble. "Be careful what you think. Sometimes it will lead you to trouble."

Mercy scowled. "He takes children from their families. No man of the cloth would proclaim that as the will of God."

Richard considered her words. It sounded so logical and correct. But who was he to judge? After the gruesome act he had committed in the cathedral. Guilt scratched the back of his mind. He shook his head. "I'm not one to ask."

A noise from down the road made Mercy turn. "The men will be back." She looked at him. "Let me come with you."

Richard began to shake his head.

"I can't stay here. Not with…" She looked back at the cottage. "…all the memories."

Richard sighed. He stared hard at her. He certainly did not want her with him. But if she was with him, he could protect her and keep her out of trouble. He cursed. "Then fetch a bag for the road and be quick about it."

She turned and raced back into the cottage.

He waited near the barn and his horse, Eoos. He grinned. It was ironic the name he had been called was the name of his horse. He patted the palfrey's neck, his mind shifting to the mission before him. He considered his options; formulated a plan. Someone knew something about where the children were being held, but they could not ask in Goodmont. Too many knew his face and Mercy's. They would have to journey to another village that worshipped at the cathedral; a village in the bishop's dioceses. Mercy would know which village to go to. Perhaps she *could* help him. He would simply have to remember that she was not to be trusted.

Just as he thought this, he smelled smoke. He looked up at the cottage to see the chickens run from the structure.

Through the gaps at the side of the curtain, he saw flames. His heart quickened and he quickly moved forward. A figure pushed the curtain aside, emerging into the morning sunlight. Her brown hair reflected the red of the snapping flames behind her as they quickly engulfed the cottage. She carried a sack over her shoulder and a piece of burning wood. She tossed the wood aside as she approached.

"What did you do?" Richard gasped as he stared at the flames eating away at the cottage.

"With any luck, they will think I died in the flames." She walked by him.

The fire spread fast. Hungry red tongues danced and ate away at the roof.

He had to admire her thinking. It would give them time.

"I only wish I could burn the village."

He glanced at her retreating form in surprise. What had they unleashed?

Chapter Eleven

"Are you sure we shouldn't go directly to the cathedral?" Mercy asked.

Richard clenched his teeth. "I agreed you could accompany me, not that you would have a say in the plan."

Mercy scowled. She slouched in the saddle of her horse. They had been riding all day. That was an entire day without Kit. Anxiety crept around her like spiders. "Maybe –"

Richard brought Eoos to a halt and glanced over his shoulder to look at her. "Should we knock on the front door and ask if they've seen the boys?"

Mercy frowned.

"We'll start in the village of Dunford. You said the village also worshipped at the cathedral. We'll ask around, subtly. See if any of their children were taken. Remember, we don't want to call attention to ourselves."

Mercy kept quiet. She bit her lip. Kit had never been away from her for an entire day. What was the bishop doing to him? "I miss him," she admitted.

Richard grunted. "It's very important you think about this question. Does anyone know you in Dunford? Is there anyone that would recognize you?"

Mercy considered his question. "No. I visited Dunford once with Dean." She looked at Richard's proud, strong back. He was so different from Eoos, the man she had cared for; the man she remembered him to be. He seemed...colder...somehow. "The question should be will anyone recognize *you*."

"Not unless they saw me at court or my home." He swiveled around to look at her. "It's not likely."

"And yet Bartholomew recognized you."

Richard seemed to consider her words. He nodded. "We'll have to be very careful. Let's get one thing straight. You are to do everything I tell you without question. Do you understand?"

Mercy grimaced.

"I'm not rescuing you if the bishop or his guards happen to see you."

"I wouldn't expect you to." Not after how she treated him. She should have told him the truth.

"Then we are in understanding."

She nodded. "All I want is my son back."

"That's what you've wanted all along."

His tone was stated as fact. There was no condemnation in it. For that, she was grateful. She knew he was angry with her. But she was angry, too. He had said he would save them. She had expected him to honor that vow. But he hadn't been there. Perhaps he was not the one who was colder, more distrustful. Maybe it was her. Maybe it was both of them.

They rode in silence for the rest of the trip until they came to Dunford. It was a bigger village than Goodmont. As they approached, the road became more crowded with merchants moving to and from the village. Thatched roofed houses lined the streets. In the distance, Mercy saw a tall spire with a cross on it. Like a beacon, it called to her.

Someone bumped her horse, and she looked down to

see a bread merchant hurrying by. Slowly, she acknowledged all the people on the road. One woman carried a child on one hip and a basket on the other. A merchant led a horse-drawn wagon filled with large empty casks away from the town. They passed a man arguing at the side of the road with another man.

Despair set over Mercy. How were they going to find Kit here? They should go directly to the cathedral.

As they neared the town, calls of merchants reached her. "Get your bread here before the sun sets!"

"Candles!"

"Thief! Someone stop him!"

Mercy saw a small boy running from an apple merchant who waved a stick above his head. The child raced across the road and toward another shop. She grinned, hoping the boy got away.

A boy! This town had children. Why was the bishop preying on her village? She watched where the boy disappeared between two buildings before turning her horse toward the merchant. She dug in her pouch and produced a coin.

The merchant's eyes glittered at the sight. "A fresh apple today?"

Mercy shook her head and pointed after the child. "That boy."

His demeanor changed instantly. His shoulders slumped, his face became hard, and his teeth clenched. He grumbled, "You know him?"

She shook her head. "Do you?"

"Pah. No. He makes trouble. That's all I know. Always trying to steal my apples. He's a homeless curmudgeon."

Mercy considered his words. *Homeless.* "Do you know where he rests for the night?"

"If I did, I would find him and have his hand cut off for the apples he steals."

Mercy sighed, rubbing the coin between her fingers

thoughtfully.

His eyes focused on the coin in her hand, greedily. "If I had to guess, I would say he lives somewhere on the north side of town. Probably gets food from the church. And my apples."

Content with the answer, Mercy tossed the coin to him. "Next time he comes by, give him an apple. Free of charge."

He caught the coin. "Yes. Of course. Of course."

Mercy steered her horse across the road, back to Richard's side, her gaze fixed on the road to the north.

Richard shook his head in displeasure. "I said to do everything I tell you."

She looked at him. "You didn't tell me to do anything."

His gaze bore into hers in warning.

She ignored the warning and jerked on the reins of her horse. "This way." She led the way north, following the road toward the roof with a cross on it. The sun was beginning to set, and the merchants were closing up their wagons and doors.

Richard moved his horse before hers, cutting off her progression. "We must find a place to rest."

She looked around his broad shoulders at the cross. "What better place than the church?"

A church.

Richard did not like her idea of hiding right beneath the bishop's nose. It was risky and dangerous. A church of all places! But he admitted to himself that they needed to rest and they could do that at the church. Perhaps the priest would have information about the boys. It was a place to start. A good place, he had to grudgingly admit.

Mercy led the way into the church. Wooden pews stretched to the front of the aisle where a table and podium stood. Behind which was a beautiful arched window that took up most of the far wall.

Tingles danced across Richard's neck. He stopped walking. He shouldn't be here.

Mercy continued on toward the front. She stopped at the first pew and genuflected.

Richard glanced around at the wooden beams far above his head and at the colorful pictures of saints on the tapestries against the side wall. It was not as big or as elaborate as Canterbury Cathedral, but it was still a holy place of worship. He didn't feel comfortable.

"Can I help you?"

Richard and Mercy turned to find a man dressed in a brown robe approaching down the aisle.

"We were hoping that you could supply a couple of travelers a warm meal," Richard said.

The priest's brown hair was peppered with strands of grey. "Of course," he agreed, clasping his hand together before him. "I have ale and…" His brow furrowed as his eyes alighted on Mercy. "Mercy?"

Mercy's mouth dropped open. "Father Stephen."

Richard tensed. Already someone recognized her! His knees bent slightly in preparation to seize Mercy and flee.

Mercy rushed by Richard and embraced the priest.

Surprised, Richard stared at the warm reunion. The tension slowly left his body and confusion washed over him. Should he run? Would this turn out bad for him?

Mercy pulled back. "I forgot you came to Dunford."

"It's good to see you," Father Stephen said. He glanced at Richard. "I hadn't heard you re-married."

"No," Richard and Mercy protested together.

"I am escorting her on her journey," Richard clarified, glancing at Mercy. It was the truth.

"Please don't ask any further questions, Father," Mercy pleaded.

Father Stephen stared at her for a long moment before

giving her a nod and a warm grin. "You are both welcome here. I've known Mercy for a long time, and I trust her." He looked at Richard.

Richard drew himself up. He didn't know the Father, and while it was obvious Mercy trusted him, Richard did not. He wasn't sure whether to tell him the truth of who he was, or lie.

Mercy hooked her arm through his. "This is Richard."

Her touch surprised him and sent an instant jolt through his body. Even though he was angry with her, his heart quickened at her touch.

Father Stephen nodded.

"One more thing," Mercy said as they walked toward the back door. "No one must know we are here."

Father Stephen smiled. "Of course not."

The cloister was a separate building near the church. It housed Father Stephen and visiting dignitaries. Luckily, there was only Father Stephen there at the moment. Mercy and Richard were given separate rooms and a warm meal. After they retired for the evening, Mercy lay on the straw mattress, staring into the darkness. It was the first time that day she was alone. Immediately, guilt settled around her like a rough blanket. She could not rest until Kit was with her, until she found him. She pushed back her fears to concentrate on what to do next. But the only thing she could think of in the dark was Kit. Where was he? What was he doing? What were they doing to him?

Frustrated and scared, she sat up as dark images danced in her mind. She had to find him! She couldn't wait here, sleeping, relaxing. Her son was in danger! She threw the blanket aside and stood. She paced, clenching and unclenching her hands. Despair rose inside her. She had failed him. She hadn't been able to protect him anymore than Abbey had her son. She clenched her teeth against the rush of uselessness that crested inside her.

With a soft cry, she rushed from the room into the corridor. Darkness. Disorientation. She walked down the hallway, down the stairs to the room they had eaten in. The small hearth still gave off warmth. She sat in a chair before it and stared into the dying flames. Was she selfish for wanting her son to stay with her? Would she be punished in the afterlife? She didn't care. The only thing she cared about was Kit. She couldn't help thinking that if the bishop was truly doing God's work with the children, why couldn't they see them or know where they were? Why did he keep it a secret? Why did he take them?

She and Kit had never been apart since the day he was born. Was he crying? Was he needing her? Mercy put her hand over her mouth to stifle a sob.

"Mercy?"

She whirled to find a shadow in the doorway. The red flickering light of the fire washed over Richard, giving him a rosy glow.

"Why are you not sleeping?"

"I can't sleep." She turned back to the fire.

Richard pulled up a chair beside her. "You should really try. You will need your strength."

"What are you doing up?"

"I heard you."

She looked at him. The firelight touched his cheeks and she remembered the fever he had endured the first night she had seen him. He looked so much better. The swelling was almost completely gone from his eye. It was as though her Eoos was gone and in his place was this stranger she didn't know. She needed Eoos. She wondered if he had risen with the intent to leave. She looked back at the fire. "You don't have to do this, you know."

"Sit beside you?"

"Look for Kit."

"No. I don't. But I am."

"Why?"

He gazed into the fire thoughtfully. "I like Kit. It troubles me that he might be in danger."

Mercy felt a wave of terror rise inside her. "What kind of danger?" Her voice trembled.

"Mercy," Richard called. When she didn't look at him, he took her hands into his. "Kit is a smart boy. I'm sure he's fine."

"No." She shook her head. "He's not. They took him from his home. They stole him from his family. He's frightened and I can't reach him. I can't find him."

Richard squeezed her hands. "We will find him." He reached back and pulled a cloak from a chair. He draped it around her shoulders. "Here." He pulled her chair closer to his and gently gathered her against him. "Close your eyes and rest."

She resisted for a moment, but she was exhausted, mentally and physically. She lay her head against his shoulder.

He stroked her arm.

His embrace eased her fears and she felt safe. "I would never have given you to the bishop."

Richard grinned against the top of her head. "You would have. And I don't blame you."

"I'm sorry I lied to you. I should have told you the truth. Told you what I knew about what you had done."

"It wouldn't have mattered. I still would have helped you."

"Why?"

"Because you were kind to me. Not many are."

"I put my needs above yours. I shouldn't have done that."

Richard squeezed her tightly. "I know why you did it. For Kit. I understand. And I was angry, but I don't fault you.

Not at all."

She looked up at him. "Are you still angry?"

"How can I still be angry with you?" He brushed a lock of her hair from her cheek.

The brush of his fingers sent shivers through her body. She sighed against him, her head and body nestling closer to his. "It doesn't matter. None of it does. You were my salvation from the moment I saw you at the inn. You were the only one who would help. Then and now." Her eyes began to close. The fire in the hearth blinking in and out of her sight.

Richard's chuckle sounded low in her ears. "You are the only one to see me in that light."

"That's because they are all fools," she whispered, and fell into an exhausted slumber.

The sound of crashing metal jarred Mercy awake.

Standing frozen near the hearth was a small, thin boy. His eyes were wide as they locked with hers. His brown hair hung over his eyes.

It took a moment for Mercy's sleep-filled mind to recognize the boy as the child stealing an apple in the market the prior day. Just as she remembered him, the boy bolted, running for the door.

"Wait!" Mercy cried. "Wait! Please! I won't hurt you!"

The boy didn't stop and dashed directly into a large form that suddenly appeared in the doorway. Richard caught the boy by the arm. The boy reacted instinctively, kicking and squirming to escape.

"Did he harm you?" Richard demanded of Mercy.

Mercy shook her head and quickly rushed to the boy. "We won't harm you."

"What do ya want?" the child growled, looking at her

suspiciously.

Mercy glanced at Richard and then back at the boy. He had fight in his brown eyes. "How was your apple?"

"Are ya goin' ta hand me over to that fat merchant? One or two apples ain't gonna harm anyone. I was just hungry!" He tugged at his arm, but Richard held him still.

"I know," Mercy said softly. "Please. I have just one question for you."

The boy's eyes narrowed distrustfully.

"Bishop Devdan."

At the bishop's name, the boy's eyes grew large. He began to pull savagely at his arm again. "Let me go!"

"He lives on his lands in a castle, near the cathedral."

"So what?" the boy snapped. "I never saw 'im. Let me go!"

His reaction was so intense and severe that Mercy knew the boy knew the bishop. "Have you been to the cathedral? Are there boys there?"

The boy scowled fiercely. He still pulled at his arm, trying to break free of Richard's hold. "I don't know nothin'."

"Don't lie, boy," Richard warned.

"I ain't no liar!" he proclaimed.

"Have you ever been to the cathedral?" Mercy asked, trying to squash the desperation she felt growing in her breast.

"No," he snapped, pouting and eyeing Richard with animosity.

He was obviously scared and dishonest. "Have you seen any boys at the cathedral?"

"No. There are no boys there. Only those monks."

"How do you know if you've never been to the cathedral?" Richard demanded. "Looks like you *are* being untruthful."

The boy's lip curled in disdain.

Mercy took a deep breath. She held up her hand to

Richard in a plea for lenience. She knelt before the boy. "Please. The bishop took my son. I'm looking for him."

The boy scowled.

"Let the child go." The voice ordered from down the corridor.

Mercy lifted her gaze to see Father Stephen approaching. Richard held the boy's arm for a second longer before releasing him. The child raced to Father Stephen who laid a calming hand on his head.

"I think there are some peas growing on the vines in the back. Go and pick some. And bring some to the others."

The boy nodded, cast a glance back at Mercy and Richard, and then ran away down the corridor.

Mercy wanted to run after him. She was certain he knew more than he was saying. But at Father Stephen's disapproving frown, she stayed where she was and try to make amends. "We weren't going to hurt him. We're sorry if we alarmed him."

"Thomas has had a difficult life. He has no home but the church. No one to watch over him." He stopped before them. "What did you want with him?"

"Where did he come from?" Richard asked.

"Come from?"

"Where are his parents?"

"I don't know. I found him in the village, starving. Afraid. I didn't ask him about his family."

"You said there were others. Other children?" Mercy wondered.

"Yes. There are four children that I know of. Dunford is a larger village than Goodmont. The children sometimes go unnoticed. Thomas is one of the oldest. He helps me look out for the others."

"Are they all boys?" Richard asked.

Mercy felt tingles along the nape of her neck.

"Yes." Father Stephen scowled. "How did you know?"

Richard met Mercy's gaze in silent revelation.

Her heart squeezed tight. Could they be children the bishop had taken from her village? From other villages? Would they know where Kit was being kept? Thomas was not from her village, but he knew the bishop. "We need to speak to Thomas."

"What is this about? You've come to Dunford for a reason. I would like to help. Is there anything I can do?" Father Stephen asked.

Mercy hesitated. Walter's betrayal was fresh in her mind. Even though she liked Father Stephen, he was a man of the cloth, like the bishop. She wasn't sure if she could trust him.

"What do you know about Bishop Devdan?" Richard asked. There was bitterness in his voice.

She looked at him, but his face was void of emotion.

"Bishop Devdan?" Father Stephen echoed.

Mercy shook her head, ready to tell Richard not to ask, not to give away their mission.

"The boy seemed to be afraid when Mercy mentioned the bishop," Richard said. "I want to know why."

Relief swept through Mercy. They could not afford for the bishop to discover them so close to his home. And she wondered how loyal Father Stephen was to the bishop. For all she knew, he could be part of the bishop's plan to steal the children. Her instincts were telling her this was not the case. Father Stephen helped the children of the village. But she couldn't be certain of his loyalties.

"Thomas is afraid of many of the men," Father Stephen explained. "He was terrified of me when we first met."

"He didn't seem to be afraid of me. He put up quite a fight," Richard replied.

Father Stephen looked from Richard to Mercy and back. "I have only respect for the bishop."

"How often does he visit Dunford?" Richard asked.

"Not often. I go to the cathedral if I need his guidance."

"You've been to the cathedral?" Mercy asked,

hopefully.

"Of course."

"What did you see?" she asked.

Father Stephen scowled at her in confusion. "It's a beautiful cathedral. Mercy, child. I don't understand what you are looking for. I want to help."

Mercy wanted to confide in him, but there was too much at stake. She looked away from Father Stephen to Richard.

"Can you escort me to the cathedral?" Richard stared at Father Stephen intensely.

"Why do you need an escort? Many go there to pray and worship. It is a house of prayer open to all."

"Can you show me around the cathedral? Perhaps point out holy artifacts or prevent me from entering somewhere I should not go."

Father Stephen nodded suspiciously. "Of course." He looked at Mercy. "Will you be joining us?"

Mercy began to nod, but Richard cut her off. "No. Not this trip. She has things to do in the village."

Mercy was going to object but thought it better to remain silent until she discovered what Richard had in mind.

"I will be ready whenever you are," Richard proclaimed.

Father Stephen nodded. "I have some duties to perform. I shall return shortly."

"Do you need any help?" Mercy offered, feeling guilty about involving him.

"Richard has already helped quite a bit this morn. But I would be grateful if you prepared dinner for tonight when we return."

"Of course, Father."

"If you'll excuse me." Father Stephen turned and moved off toward the church.

When he was out of sight, Richard guided Mercy out of

the hallway, back into the kitchen.

"I want to go with you," Mercy objected in a quiet voice.

"No. I will search the cathedral. You need to stay here and find Thomas. Ask him about his family. Where he came from. Where he met the other children. There may be more information there."

Mercy was torn. She wanted desperately to go with them and search the cathedral. But if Richard was right, the boys might have information about the bishop. She had a horrible feeling of anxiety. "I don't think we should split up."

Richard's look softened. He glanced back at the door.

Mercy thought he heard something, until he turned back to her.

He pulled her against him and lowered his lips to hers. He held her tightly, brushing his lips across hers, teasing her with flicks of his tongue. She sighed softly and he swept into her mouth, deepening the kiss.

Swirls of desire flooded her, and she embraced him, pulling him close. Her body came alive, igniting with need.

Richard gently pulled back, gazing into her eyes. "I'll be back. I promise." He stepped away from her and steadied her with a hand at her waist, before leaving.

Mercy stared after him. A whirlwind tossed her mind about. She blinked. He was no longer her Eoos. The commanding kiss was powerful and expert. He had found himself. A confident knight of the realm.

Chapter Twelve

Richard dismounted his horse behind Father Stephen. He had convinced Father Stephen to loan him a robe to wear in the hopes no one would recognize him. It was a little too short, but it would do. Mercy had done an adequate job of darkening and cutting his hair, and he had shaved. He hoped it was enough to keep from being identified.

The cathedral rose far above his head, and bells rang out. It reminded him of a smaller Canterbury Cathedral. He pushed the images and thoughts aside. He was here only to find Kit.

Father Stephen pointed to the tall tower where a large cross was situated. "That was struck by lightning two years ago. Bishop Devdan had it replaced."

Richard stared up at the cross. "Isn't that an ill omen?"

Father Stephen shrugged. "Many saw it as such. Now that it is replaced, the talk of evil and omens has died down."

Not by all, Richard thought. He followed Father Stephen toward the door. If he could only find Kit. He longed to see Mercy smile and hold her child. He wanted her to be happy. Despite her dishonesty about his identity, he admired her. She was steadfast in her concern and protection for her boy. He couldn't explain it, but he wanted to please her. He wanted to remain at her side even though he knew she would hand him over to the bishop to get Kit back.

Father Stephen pushed the door open. He stepped into the corridor that was lit by tall windows on either side of the door. "This way leads to the cathedral. That to the monastery."

"The monks all serve the bishop?" Richard asked, peering down the corridor toward the monastery.

"We all serve the Lord," Father Stephen replied. He nodded to a monk who passed them from the cathedral, heading toward the monastery.

Richard was surprised at his answer. He followed him down the corridor. "As a servant of the Lord, if you saw something…" He gaged his words. Father Stephen might be loyal to the bishop. He might not know what the bishop was doing with the children. But Richard did. "…*suspicious*, you would be required to report it."

"Suspicious?" Father Stephen stopped and turned. "Probably not. Proof would be required. Are you referring to something in particular?"

"No. No." Richard ran a hand through his hair. "It's just that you say your loyalty is to God."

"It is."

"And yet, men are fallible. Human. Any man can be corrupted."

"We all do our best. I am not here to judge."

"If you're not here to judge, how could you report evil if you saw it? How would you know it if you saw it?"

"Evil?"

Richard nodded.

"God guides us all. I hope he would give me the courage to do the right thing." Father Stephen pointed to a small statue in an alcove on the wall. "This is Abraham. God ordered him to sacrifice his only son."

Richard stared at the small statue of an elderly man looking up toward the sky with a young boy at his side. "The story of Abraham was never one I understood. Why would God tell Abraham to sacrifice his only son? Why would Abraham do it?"

"God wanted Abraham to prove himself loyal. He wanted Abraham to prove he placed his faith in God completely above all else, even his own son."

Richard ran a finger along the boy statue's head. "And what of the boy? What of the child? He was just a pawn?"

"The child was saved. God did not have Abraham harm him."

Richard couldn't stop thinking of Kit. "The child was innocent," he whispered. "Scared. It wasn't fair to him." He shook himself and looked toward the monastery. "Are there any boys here, at the cathedral?"

"I have never seen any children here."

Richard turned to the statue. The children should never be sacrificed. They were innocent. Unlike Bishop Devdan. Why he hadn't known the bishop taking the children was Devdan until recently, escaped him. He couldn't remember Mercy voicing the bishop's name. But once he got his memory back and realized who the bishop was, everything fell into place. Now, there was an urgency to find Kit.

When he looked at Father Stephen, Richard found him gazing at him in thoughtfulness. "Shall we continue?" Richard asked.

The Father nodded and continued toward the cathedral.

Mercy didn't wait long after Richard and Father Stephen left before beginning her search for Thomas. She scoured the church thinking the boy would remain close for safety and for food. When she couldn't find him, she remembered she had first seen him in the village near the apple merchant. After exploring the church, she went into the village.

Dunford was a busy village, the main road lined with merchants and buyers. It was crowded, and she stepped to the side of the candle maker's shop to watch the throngs of people in the street, some riding horses, some on carts, many on foot. Mercy realized she would never find Thomas if he didn't want to be found. There were too many places for him to hide.

She stopped at the apple merchant's wagon.

He smiled as she approached, and held out an apple. "I have not seen the little runt today."

She handed him a coin and took the apple. "Thank you."

Then, she remembered the merchant told her that Thomas must live on the north side of the town. She headed back toward the church. She happened to glance back at the town to find the apple merchant speaking with two soldiers. Shivers of apprehension raced down her spine when the merchant pointed his cane at her.

She turned and hurriedly moved away from the main street. The crowd thinned and she expected the soldiers to come after her at any moment. She cut through a farmer's wheat field, chancing a glance over her shoulder. The street remained empty. She breathed a small sigh of relief. She was being foolish. They didn't know her in Dunford. Who knew what the merchant was speaking with them about. She needed to focus on her mission of finding Thomas. She neared a farmer's house made of wattle and daub. It was quiet except for a bird chirping. The golden field of wheat swayed gently in the breeze.

A child would need protection from nature, from the rain. Perhaps she should search for a run down, empty house? Or a cave?

She heard the clank of a blacksmith's shop as she came to the house. It stopped suddenly when the pounding of hooves sounded. Instinctively, Mercy ducked behind the mud wall of the farmer's house. After a moment, as the sound grew, she chanced a look around the side of the house.

A dusty cloud rose from the road and Mercy could see two horses galloping along it. They stopped at the edge of the field of wheat where she had entered. A path of crushed wheat led to her. They glanced toward the farmhouse and she pulled back. They must be looking for her!

Father Stephen had led Richard through the cathedral. There had been no sign of any children, only glassy-eyed saints staring at him with recrimination. The longer he stayed, the more uneasy and anxious he became. He interrupted Father Stephen's tour. "May I see the monastery?"

Father Stephen's eyes narrowed slightly. "Are you searching for something in particular?"

Richard studied a statue of St. Paul, a bearded prophet holding a sword in one hand and a bible in the other. "I am considering a life in the holy order," he lied. The saints were already looking at him with displeasure. What was a little lying in a cathedral in comparison to his past sins?

Father Stephen's eyebrows rose in surprise. "You should speak with Abbot Luke. He can guide you better than I."

Richard nodded but immediately regretted his words. He wanted as few people as possible to know he was here. He was afraid someone would recognize him. As they walked toward the front of the cathedral, down the corridor, he heard muted talking. Nothing wrong with that in a cathedral or monastery. But then, he heard something that made him pause. He reached out and clasped Father Stephen's arm.

The clink of armor echoed through the corridor.

"I would like to pray for direction before I speak to the Abbot." He stepped back, casting a wary eye down the hallway.

"Of course." Father Stephen turned.

Richard wished he had a sword. If this was the bishop's soldiers, he would have nothing to defend himself with. His best options were to stay hidden or run. He couldn't help Kit if he was in the dungeon…or worse.

He returned to the cathedral and paused, glancing back down the hallway before he entered. He expected knights to come rushing down the corridor to apprehend him. He was being foolish, he knew. How would they know he was here? Unless… His gaze snapped to Father Stephen.

"You wanted to pray…?" Father Stephen encouraged uneasily.

Furious, Richard grabbed him and slammed him up against the wall. "Do you know who I am?"

"You are Richard!" Father Stephen exclaimed.

Richard pushed his face closer, snarling, "Do you know who I am?"

"Yes! Yes! Sir Richard le Breton! Yes! I know."

"You contacted the bishop. You told the soldiers."

"I sent word to the bishop. Yes!"

Richard growled softly. He should have known the church was no sanctuary for him. But it wasn't him he was concerned about. "Mercy. Is she in danger?" His fingers curled into the Father's robe.

"No," he said quickly. "I would never do that to her."

"You already have. She is searching for her son! The bishop took him from her. If he knows I'm here, he knows she is." Richard tossed Father Stephen aside and hurried into the cathedral. There had to be another way out. He paused and looked back at the Father who was slowly standing. "How do I get out?"

Father Stephen appeared frail and shaken, frightened. He pointed to the altar.

Richard hurried across the stone floor of the cathedral to the altar. Suddenly, soldiers rushed into the cathedral. He raced behind the altar, searching for a door, a passageway, anything to escape. He couldn't find a doorway. Had Father Stephen lied to trap him for the bishop?

"There! There!" The soldiers raced up the center aisle.

Grimacing, Richard desperately scanned the wall behind the altar. He stepped back, turning to search the room for another way out. That was when he noticed the hallway off to the side. He rushed toward it...

...only to be greeted by more guards. He was trapped.

Mercy's heart pounded. Where could she run to escape the soldiers? She had to escape! She moved to the opposite side of the farmer's house, searching for a tree or brush that would offer her cover.

"This way!"

The soldiers were coming closer. They couldn't catch her! She had to be free to find Kit! There was no cover across the farmlands. If she ran, they would see her. No cover on the road. She turned the corner, pressing herself up against the wall of the house.

"Go around. I'll go this way."

No, Mercy thought. She would not let them find her. She stumbled over a branch. She reached down to grasp it, preparing to use it as a weapon. A hand shot out and wrapped around her wrist. Startled, she jumped back.

Mercy saw Thomas tucked under a bush near the

bottom of the house. It appeared he was beneath the house. He pressed a finger to his lips and signaled for her to come with him. He moved the bush aside and Mercy quickly slid down to where he was.

Darkness engulfed her.

Thomas pushed the bush back into place. Together, they huddled beneath the house, behind the bush in the quiet dark, watching. It was only a few moments later that footsteps sounded and the light from between the branches of the bush was broken by shadows.

Mercy pulled back, hoping the soldiers wouldn't find them in the hole.

"Where did she go?"

"Into the house." The guards moved away. There was a pounding that sounded further away.

Thomas took Mercy's hand and led her deeper beneath the house, into the darkness. It wasn't a hole. It was some sort of tunnel. Mercy had to crawl as she followed Thomas. She couldn't stand because the passageway was too small. Thomas crawled beside her. The small tunnel seemed to go on forever. She thought she heard other rustlings behind her. She was grateful that Thomas was with her. But where was he taking her? It had to be better than being caught by the bishop's soldiers.

Thomas moved in front of her as the passageway narrowed. Pebbles and small rocks were scattered in the dirt of the passageway. Mercy's palms and knees repeatedly fell on them as she crawled forward. She ignored the pinch of pain and continued after Thomas. Her hands brushed over dirt. She adjusted her skirt repeatedly so she wouldn't trip over it. "Thomas," she whispered.

"Shhh," Thomas answered quietly, quickly.

The darkness was complete, surrounding her in nothingness. Panic ate away at the borders of her sanity as her mind began to play tricks on her. She felt something slide over her hand, and she yanked it back. She heard the soft rumble of dirt collapsing and hurried after Thomas. Where were they going? What if she lost him? Would she stumble around in the darkness forever? She pushed the swelling terror aside. At least the soldiers wouldn't find her. But would she survive?

The air was stale and heavy. She took a deep breath and got a mouthful of dust. She coughed hard.

In front of her, Thomas paused until her fit of coughing stopped. "We're almost there," he whispered. "Put one of your hands over your mouth."

Mercy did as he directed, but it didn't help much because she had to use it to crawl forward. They moved quietly then. Mercy followed him, knowing the end would be coming soon. The tunnel was longer than the farmhouse and she wondered where the end would be. Or maybe it was her mind wishing to be free of the confinement. What if the cave collapsed? What if they were trapped? Shivers of anxiety and dread danced across her back. Just as she thought she could take no more, just as the fear was about to take over, she saw a light ahead. At first, she thought it was a reflection or a play of her mind. But as they neared, the light increased. She saw that the tunnel, and yes, that was what she was in, opened ahead. She had never been so grateful to see light before. A wave of fresh air moved over her like a wave. She inhaled deeply and let out a little sigh.

Thomas paused to look back at her.

Now she knew why he looked so dirty. He crawled around in these caves. "I'm alright," she admitted with gratitude.

He moved forward until he fell from the opening, his body disappearing before her. Then, he reappeared, standing.

When Mercy came to the opening, Thomas held a hand out to help her. A small cave opened before her. It was an enclosed cave with small animal bones and blankets and debris scattered about on the floor. Two other holes just like the one she crawled out through were on the cave wall. Escape routes, she guessed. This was his home. This was why no one could ever find him.

She took Thomas's hand and he helped her out of the tunnel. When her feet touched the floor, she dusted off her dress and mumbled a thank you to Thomas. Three other boys stood huddled together near one of the holes, eyeing Mercy with distrust. They were just as dusty as Thomas and wore ragged clothing. They seemed to be around the same age as Thomas.

Her gaze moved over the boys. One looked as though he was going to dive into the hole and scurry away at any moment. These were the other boys Father Stephen spoke about. She grinned, greeting them, "Good day."

None of them replied.

She glanced at Thomas. "Thank you for your help."

Thomas shrugged. "'twas nothin'. The bishop's men were after ya. Anyone who is an enemy of the bishop is our friend."

That seemed to relax the boy about to run. He ran a dirty sleeve across his nose. He was the smallest one. He was thin, his clothing hanging off his body. His dark hair hung over his eyes as if he were hiding from someone.

Mercy's gaze took in the other two children. The one in the center had his arms crossed. He had brown hair and a blackened eye. Was he a fighter as Richard was, or had some adult done this to him?

Her gaze moved to the other boy. His eyes were dark, and his lips were a thin slash. His hair was pushed back from his face. Mercy gasped slightly. She knew him! His face was thinner than she remembered, and longer, older. She took a step closer to look into his eyes. Older eyes, but still a child. "Rafe?"

Distrust and apprehension filled his eyes. He took a step away from her.

"It's me. Mercy. Mercy Brooker."

His eyes narrowed as his gaze swept over her. "Mercy?"

She nodded. "I'm Kit's mother. Do you remember me?"

A moment passed in which she thought she could be wrong. Maybe this wasn't Rafe. But then, his eyes widened. "Yes! I remember you! I remember! I used ta play with Kit! You lived in the same village as me! Can you take me home?"

Her heart ached. Rafe! He had been taken four years before Kit, just before Dean's death. "Yes!" Overjoyed, she stepped forward to embrace him, but he pulled away from her quickly. She froze, staring in shock. What had happened to him? What had the bishop done? She nodded, trying to reassure him without touching him. "It's alright. I'll take you home."

Hesitant and fearful, his stare swept over her. He nodded and kept his distance.

He wasn't the carefree, happy child she remembered, the young boy who had played with Kit. Kit! Rafe would know where he was. "Have you seen Kit?"

Rafe shook his head.

"Where did the bishop take you?"

"Why didn't ya stop him?" Thomas demanded. "Why did ya let him take Rafe?"

"I couldn't," Mercy replied, but at his accusation, a dagger of repentance and horror sliced through her. "I couldn't stop him. The bishop is very powerful. He has soldiers." She sighed softly. "I'm sorry. I would have if I could." She dropped to her knees before Rafe. "I'm sorry."

Rafe nodded but wouldn't look at her.

"I will bring you home." She looked down at the ground, at the ripped blankets strewn about. "But I have to find Kit first."

"Can't you take me home first?" Rafe asked.

"It's not safe. The bishop might go back to Goodmont. If he found you –"

Rafe's scowl was fierce and angry. "I'm not going back with him."

"I will take you home. I promise. When it's safe."

"It will never be safe. I escaped once. He would never let me escape again."

"We all escaped," Thomas proclaimed proudly, lifting his chin in defiance.

"From where?" she demanded. Because that was where Kit was. "Where did the bishop keep you?"

"The castle."

"On the hill," Rafe added.

"He keeps us prisoner there."

Bishop Devdan's castle. It wasn't far. The boys could have escaped and come here to find safety. He kept them prisoner? That wasn't what he told the village. "Did he hurt you?"

They looked from one to the other and then down at the floor. "No," Thomas said for all of them.

She didn't believe him. There was something in the way he answered that was practiced, fake. She clenched her teeth. "I'm going there. I'm going to get the rest of the boys."

"No!" Thomas said. He shook his head frantically. "You won't come back."

Sympathy swept through her. How much agony had they known? "Did the bishop take you from your family?"

Thomas scowled. "Me mum sold me ta 'im."

Mercy was horrified. What kind of mother would sell her son? "As a slave? What did the bishop do with you?"

Thomas looked down; his lips pursed.

Mercy looked at the other boys.

Rafe scowled fiercely and the other boys looked away.

"It's alright. It doesn't matter," Mercy told them. "You don't have to tell me." It was enough that they were prisoners. She didn't need to know the horrors they went through. "It's alright."

How was she to get to the castle without being noticed?

She looked at Thomas. Then her gaze swept Rafe and the other two children. They had escaped. They would know how to get in. She dropped to her knees before Thomas. "He has my boy. I have to go to the castle and find him. I have to find Kit."

Thomas shook his head in disapproval.

"It's not just Kit. There are others there," Rafe said quietly.

Mercy looked at him over her shoulder. "How many?"

"I don't know. We were never allowed to see each other."

"They kept us in separate small rooms. Until the bishop wanted us," Thomas said quietly.

Like animals, Mercy thought.

"There was one time he brought us out. He made us line up," Rafe said. "I remember how happy I was ta see the sun. There were maybe six or seven others."

Thomas nodded, but there was no happiness in his face. Only a haunting coldness.

Mercy swallowed. "Thomas. Rafe. You escaped. How did you do it?"

Rafe and Thomas exchanged uneasy glances. "I used to go exploring at night," Thomas said quietly.

"If you were bad, the bishop would make sure you had a guard," Rafe explained. "Or if there were visitors. The bishop didn't want us seen. He would make sure we didn't leave our rooms by putting a guard there."

Thomas nodded. "In the beginning, you have an escort. Until you get used to the rules."

"But you are not allowed to leave your room. Ever."

Both boys were silent for a long moment, remembering.

Mercy looked at the younger boys sitting on the floor. "What if you were caught?" she wondered.

"You were punished," the smallest boy whispered. It sounded like a shout in the small cave. He sat in the corner of the cavity; his knees pulled up to his chest.

Both Thomas and Rafe looked at the boy.

"They caught him out at night once," Thomas said quietly.

Rafe went and sat next to the boy. He looked at Mercy. "Will was in the room next to mine." He looked back at the small boy. "We talked through a hole in the wall. I promised him I wouldn't leave without him."

The boy nodded, looking at Rafe with adoration. "And ya took me with."

Rafe nodded, a strange grin on his face.

Mercy's heart twisted. How many other boys were like Will? Punished. Hurt. What did the bishop do to them?

Thomas sneezed twice and then dusted his shirt off. "I started sneaking out of my room at night ta find a way out. I finally did. Through the crypts."

"The crypts?"

"Where they keep all the dead of the castle. I think the bishop's mom and dad are down there."

"Can we get into the castle that way?"

Thomas shook his head. "I'm not goin' back."

Mercy couldn't blame him. She didn't want them to go back. She didn't want them in danger. "No. You don't have to. I just need someone to show me how to get in."

Rafe looked at all the boys.

"I would never ask you to go back into the castle. It's too dangerous. But I have to. I have to find Kit."

"There are other boys like us," Rafe said. "They're prisoners there."

"It's not our concern," Thomas stated strongly. "We got out."

Rafe looked at Will. Finally, he stood. "I'll show you how I escaped. I'll show you where to go."

Chapter Thirteen

𝕴n a large room in Devdan Castle, Richard was shoved to his knees by two guards. His hands were bound behind him. A large wooden cross hung on the wall before him.

"Sir Richard le Breton," a voice said from the darkness. Clunk. Shuffle. Clunk.

Richard's lip was cut where a guard had punched him. He had been overpowered in the cathedral by the bishop's soldiers.

"Have you come to put a sword through *my* head?" the bishop asked.

If only he could. If only his hands were free. He needed no sword to end this Satan's spawn's life. But he remained silent.

"You have no words for me?"

"I have many words for you. None you would like to hear."

The bishop emerged from a dark corner of the large room in his white vestments. "You dare to enter a holy place of worship after what you did?"

It was a statement that required no response from Richard, and he kept his mouth closed.

"What were you doing there? Seeking repentance?"

Richard kept his head bowed, even as his teeth clenched and his hands fisted.

"Or were you looking for something? Or someone?"

He knew! Devdan knew why he was here. He knew that Richard was looking for the boy.

"Where is the woman?"

"If you're looking for a woman, you are in the wrong profession."

The bishop's eyes narrowed on his thin face. "What was her name? Mercy Brooker."

Dread sliced through Richard. He hoped Mercy was nowhere near this castle or the bishop. But he had been betrayed by that priest, so she must have been also. "I don't know her."

"More lies?" Clunk. Shuffle. Clunk. "I shouldn't be surprised. Not from one such as you."

Taunts would not work with him. It had been eighteen months since the murder of Becket. He had grown used to them from knights and peasants alike. "What do you want with me?"

"The murderer of the Archbishop Thomas Becket?" The bishop laughed and it came out as a high-pitched crazy sound. "I could execute you and be called a hero."

"I don't think anyone would call you a hero. Child-stealer, maybe."

The bishop's laughter suddenly stopped. "We all have our crosses to bear."

"Where do you keep the boys?"

"They perform God's work. Even the innocent must labor in the service of our Lord. That is something you know nothing about. Heretic."

"Is that what you plan to do? Bore me with your insults?"

The bishop's lips thinned. "You should speak to me with reverence. Do you know who I am?"

Richard slowly lifted his gaze to the bishop. "I know who you are." His lips curled in disdain. "When I was young, a younger man, really only a boy, told me about a priest. A priest who...did things to him. Touched him in inappropriate ways. Made him touch the priest. He told me the priest's name and I have never forgotten it." Richard's lips twitched with anger. "Tell me. How is that God's work?"

Devdan sighed softly. "I repent and am forgiven every night."

Richard shot to his feet. "You have no intention of repenting! You use those children for your repugnant sexual urges."

The bishop tapped his golden rod.

"Power has corrupted you."

"You are not one to judge. Not after what you did. At least I will be forgiven for my sins. But you cannot receive any of the sacraments. You will die and burn in Hell."

"I'll see you there."

The bishop glared at him. "I would take great pleasure in executing you."

"Stand in line."

Devdan took a deep breath. "All things in good time. I may yet have use for you."

"I wonder if the Archbishop knows what you do."

A cold grin spread across the bishop's twisted lips. "Who would dare tell him? He would never believe *you*."

Someone had to stop him. Someone had to stand up to him. But he was careful. He never chose families who had money. He preyed on those weaker than him, those who were vulnerable and afraid, those who would give up a child to remain in good standing with the church. Maybe even an entire town made up of peasants like those in Goodmont.

"You know it's true. Good. Guards!"

The men returned and laid hands on Richard.

"Take him to the dungeon. I will decide what to do with him."

The moon shone high above. Thick shadows stretched throughout the forest. Mercy ducked behind the dense brush with Rafe.

She had gone to the church earlier, searching for Richard. She was afraid to enter the church; afraid the guards would go there looking for her. Instead, she had waited outside the church, hidden. Richard had not returned. Fear and anxiety gnawed inside her. Did the bishop have Richard? She knew it was foolish to go to the cathedral. Another possibility taunted her. Had Richard decided not to help her find Kit? No. He would never do that.

Either way, she vowed to continue alone. She would find her son. Still, she was worried for Richard. He would have been here if he could.

"We have to cross the valley to get to the castle. There is no place to hide until we reach the castle," Rafe whispered.

Mercy glanced across the expanse that lay before the castle. Open field. "You don't have to do this, Rafe. Just point to where the entrance is."

Rafe shook his head as he stared out across the open field. "This is the easy part. There are guards on the walkways. They move around the castle. If we time it right…"

Mercy grasped his arm. "I mean it, Rafe."

"I want ta help. I know my mum looked for me, too." He gazed at her with such vulnerability that Mercy felt a tug at her heart. "You have ta come back. You promised to bring me home."

Mercy nodded. "Alright. But I don't want you going into the castle. Just to the entrance."

"You remember what I told you? Which floor they are on. How to get there."

Mercy nodded again. Rafe had gone over the layout of the castle with her until she saw it in her mind. "I remember."

Her gaze focused on the dark castle, cast in moonlight. Through the crenels, she saw shadowy forms of the guards moving along the walkways. Her heart pounded. She was mad for attempting this, sneaking into a castle to steal her boy from a powerful bishop. Stealing her child back from a man who was not holy.

She could not sit and do nothing. And she would not end up like Abbey. Richard had given her hope.

Was she endangering Kit by attempting to take them all? How could she not? How could she leave any of the boys? She glanced at Rafe next to her. He had escaped. And he had endured more than she knew, more than he was willing to tell her. But there were others who had not escaped.

She would find Kit first. She would make sure he was safe. Then she would save the others.

"Now!" Rafe whispered. He lurched out from behind the bush and dashed across the field.

Mercy jolted. Rafe had taken two steps before she acted. She sprinted across the valley to the side of the castle. She followed his lead, huddling next to the cold stone wall of the castle. Stone piles lined the bottom.

Rafe bent to the ground and removed one of the stones at the base of the castle.

Mercy glanced up at the crenel above them. No movement.

He quickly shoved another stone aside.

She watched him work. It took a moment before she realized he was searching for something. The entrance. He moved another stone. She knelt at his side and began moving the large rocks. All she saw was the wall of the castle meeting the ground.

Rafe sat back with a scowl. He looked over his shoulder at the valley and then back at the castle wall.

Mercy glanced up at the crenel again. Their time was running out.

He skootched to his left and began removing stones again.

Desperate, Mercy joined him. There were so many stones lining the bottom of the castle. Moments ticked by. Desperation clawed at Mercy. The entrance had to be here. Mercy's hands burned where the stones scratched her skin.

"Here!" Rafe whispered.

Mercy moved to his side and began clearing rocks. She saw a black, dark opening. It wasn't very big, and she wondered if she could fit into it.

Rafe crawled forward, moving into the darkness.

Glancing up at the crenel again, Mercy spied movement. She dove into the tiny opening. Blackness engulfed her. Thomas's cave came to mind. Another cave? Dread filled her, but she inched forward. The space was tight around her body. She felt the edge of the wall opening with her hands and moved forward. Suddenly, her hips caught, and she could go no further. She wiggled her hips, twisting them. She could feel fresh air around her calves and feet, and realized they were still out of the castle. On the other side, her head and torso were through the wall and dangling. But her hips wouldn't move. She was stuck!

Chapter Fourteen

The cell was dark. No light permeated the thick blackness. The heavy manacles around Richard's wrist itched. The cut on his lip burned. But he didn't alleviate either of them. Not by scratching or rubbing. He simply endured them. Penance, he wondered. No. It kept his mind occupied. Otherwise, his mind would wander to a desperate beautiful woman. Had they found her? Was she imprisoned somewhere in this castle?

He was useless! He drove his fist into the moist stone wall with a grunt of frustration.

Something scurried in the darkness.

He couldn't even protect the woman he loved. Loved? The word caught him off guard. Surprised, he considered it. Is that why she plagued him so? Is that why he couldn't erase the image of her blue eyes from his mind? Her soft skin still haunted his fingertips. He rubbed them together. Was that why he didn't tell the bishop she was in the town? He could have bargained with her whereabouts to gain his freedom, but he hadn't. The thought hadn't even crossed his mind.

How foolish he had been for not realizing how he felt

about her earlier. Now, she could be in danger. She *was* in danger; he was certain of it. He had to get free. He had to save her.

But how? What had the bishop wanted of him? To execute him? No. He would have done that already. No, he said he might have further use of him.

The thought repulsed him. Did he think to use him as he did the boys? No. The bishop's tastes were not for mature men.

Kit. He had to find the boy. He had to get him far away from the bishop.

There had to be something he could bargain with. Some way to get out of the dungeon.

Mercy was the only thing that came to mind. He sighed and sat back. What help was he to her? He hoped she was far from Devdan Castle. But he knew she wasn't. And that thought sent cold shivers through his body.

"I'm stuck!" Mercy whispered frantically.

In the gloom of the crypt, she saw a shadow move. Something closed over her wrist. She almost cried out until she realized it was Rafe. He began to tug at her arm. She swiveled her hips and kicked her feet to get through the tiny opening. She sucked in her stomach and pushed against the wall that held her tightly like a fisted hand. This would not stop her, she vowed. She had to get into the castle. She pushed and groaned softly.

Rafe pulled her. He placed a foot against the wall and tugged.

She heard a ripping sound and then she was flying through the air. She landed hard on a dusty floor on top of Rafe. She sat up quickly, apologizing, "I'm sorry. Are you alright?"

"Aye. Are you?" Rafe asked.

"Aye." She looked up at the hole about three feet from the ground. She had done it! *They* had done it! They were in.

Both quickly scrambled to their feet. Mercy could hardly see. Torchlight from a stairway down the hall was the only light. She wondered how he had found the exit. How he had managed to escape in such darkness. But as they walked toward the torchlight, she looked over her shoulder. Moonlight shone in through the hole in the wall. Mercy grinned. Rafe was smart and lucky. She had to admire him.

She reached out and captured his arm. "Rafe. I'm in. You should leave. I can do it."

There was silence for a moment before Rafe answered, "I keep thinking of Will. The other boys will be just as afraid as he was."

Compassion filled Mercy. If anything happened to Rafe, she would never forgive herself.

"I'm going with you."

Mercy opened her mouth to object but then closed it. He could guide her. "If anything happens, if we are caught, I want you to run. Don't worry about me. I want you to escape." She couldn't see whether he nodded or not.

He reached back and put his hand in hers before leading her to the stairway. He paused there and both of them looked toward the stairs. He waited only a moment before continuing up.

Tingles of trepidation shot across Mercy's spine. She was no spy. This was so out of the ordinary for her. She hoped the bishop underestimated the lengths she would go through to get her son back. She hoped he was not as smart as she was. She hoped... Kit and Richard were alright.

She squeezed Rafe's hand. He looked up at her. Shadows played across his face and his eyes were wide. Mercy wished he didn't have to be here with her. She wished he had never been taken. She wished the bishop had never set foot in their village. The only thing she wanted right now was to make sure the ones she loved were safe.

She nodded to Rafe, and together they moved to the top of the stairs.

Rafe put a finger to his lips and listened for a moment. Then, he looked out of the opening first one way and then the other. He stepped out.

Mercy followed him into a corridor. They hurried down the hallway. Just a few torches in sconces on the wall lit the way. It was still dark but not as dark as the crypts.

He ducked into a spiral stairway and started up. Mercy followed. He paused at the top, listening, before continuing up to the next floor.

Mercy glanced out onto the floor. It was a wide-open room, empty. She followed Rafe up the stairs until he stopped at the next floor.

"He'll be down here. But there might be a guard at his room," Rafe whispered.

Mercy felt her world spin. She was so close. How could she overpower a guard?

He looked out from the shelter of the stairway and quickly ducked back. He nodded.

She considered her options. She could... hit the guard over the head with... she looked around, but there was nothing except cold stone walls. She could...

"I'll distract him," Rafe whispered.

"No," Mercy gasped.

"Get as many boys as you can. You remember the way back?"

"Rafe," she whispered. She was supposed to be the adult. She was supposed to come up with the plans. And yet, here she was depending on a boy. A young boy who had already experienced so much trauma. "No." She grasped his arm tightly. "We'll think of something else."

"I know this castle. One guard won't be able to catch

me."

Her fingers squeezed his arm. "I won't leave you here."

He grinned. "I know." And he ran out into the corridor.

Mercy watched him hesitate and freeze. He then turned and ran down the corridor, away from the guard. Mercy pressed herself into the shadows on the wall. The guard ran past the stairway, chasing Rafe.

Mercy waited for a moment and then looked out of the stairway after the guard and Rafe. Neither was in view. She hurried to the first door. She wasn't sure which door the soldier had stood guard at. She opened the door, calling softly, "Kit?"

There was no answer.

She moved across the corridor to the next door and opened the door. "Kit?"

A small boy appeared from the darkness of the room, but he was not Kit. She beckoned for him to follow her with a wave of her hand. "Come on. We're leaving." The child stood unsurely.

Unable to take a moment to reassure him, Mercy moved to the next door and opened it. "Kit?" Without waiting for a response, she walked to the next door and the next. Until all the doors in the hallway were open. Then she turned around.

From each room, a child, a boy emerged. They eyed her with fear and with uncertainty.

Mercy's gaze swept the corridor, her gaze searching each of the faces. Kit was not there. Her heart stopped and a pain gripped her chest.

"Mom?"

She whirled. Kit stood behind her. With a strangled cry, she ran to him and embraced him, kissing his head and cheeks over and over. "Oh, Kit," she said with relief. She had thought deep down that she would never see him again. But here he was, in her arms. She pulled back to look him in his beautiful blue eyes in relief and desperation. Part of her couldn't believe she had found him. Part of her knew she would. "We're leaving." She looked back at the boys. "All of us. I know a way out."

Chapter Fifteen

Mercy led the boys down the hallway and into the stairway, keeping a tight grip on Kit's hand. She was never, ever going to let him go. She paused on the first floor and listened. When she heard no movement or speaking, she glanced out into the large room. Again, it was empty. She hoped the bishop was having a fitful sleep. She urged the boys down the stairway. There were ten of them -- some older, all between five summers and ten. Five years. The bishop had been stealing boys for five years. The thought made her ill, but she pushed it aside to concentrate on freeing the boys.

She followed them into the darkness, instructing them to hold hands. No one would be left behind. She wondered where Rafe was and checked over her shoulder to see if he was coming.

When she reached the bottom floor, the darkness was so complete, she couldn't see. She paused for a moment at the bottom of the stairs, giving her eyes time to adjust. She searched for the moonlight that she had seen shining in from the hole in the wall.

"Mom?"

"It's alright, Kit," she whispered.

She took a step forward and her foot kicked something across the floor. It rolled, clunking, until it came to a stop somewhere in the dark. Prickles shot down her spine. She didn't want to know what that had been.

She spotted the small ray of moonlight shining in through the wall and hurried forward, guiding the children. She paused just before the hole. "Here. This opening leads to the outside." She looked over her shoulder at the shadows illuminated by the flickering light of the torch in the stairway, checking to make sure they had not been followed. "You will all fit. I did."

None of the boys moved forward.

"Kit," Mercy said. "You go first. Show them it's alright."

"No. I don't want to leave you."

Mercy knelt and cupped his face in her hands, her heart squeezing. "You have to. Be brave."

He shook his head.

Mercy was so grateful she had found him. "We have to get these boys home." She pressed a kiss to his head and stood. Urgency tickled her body. She knew her time was running out. They had to get away from the castle before sunup. She picked Kit up. He clung to her and she held him for a moment. Then she held him up to the hole.

Kit crawled into the opening with ease, like a small mouth had gobbled him up.

Mercy leaned into the hole. "Kit?" There was no answer. Panic began to gnaw at her. "Kit?" she asked with desperation.

"I'm here. I'm outside."

Relief swept through her. Suddenly, the boys crowded forward, scrambling for the hole.

"One at a time," Mercy said. She picked up one boy and helped him into the hole. Another child didn't need help and went in after him. They clustered around her, desperate for freedom. She hurriedly helped another into the opening. "It's alright," she whispered. "Don't push."

One of the children suddenly screamed.

Startled, Mercy ran to him. It was difficult to see in the dark, but she saw a shadow on the floor. She reached for him and her hand brushed his shoulder. "What's wrong?"

"There!" He pointed to the floor.

In a ray of moonlight from the hole, she saw a skull on the floor. It must have been what she kicked when she entered. She pushed it gently into the darkness with her foot so none of the others saw it. "It's alright. Hurry." She gathered him to her, pulling him toward the opening and helping him into the hole.

"Stop!"

Mercy whirled toward the stairs to see Rafe run into the darkness toward them. "Hurry!" she told the children. There were only three remaining, but guards were coming. They needed to get out. Another child hurried into the hole.

Rafe reached her side. Together, they turned back to see guards tramping down the stairs.

Another boy climbed into the hole. Mercy helped the last boy.

The guards stepped into the crypts, calling, "Who's there? Halt!"

Mercy pushed Rafe toward the opening, hoping the guards didn't see the light of the moon shining through the hole. Hoping they only heard movement. Rafe disappeared into the opening.

Mercy didn't wait. She went right in after him. She inched forward until she was halfway in. She pushed forward until her torso was outside, until she could feel the air of freedom against her cheeks; she could see the boys clustered around the opening.

Rafe was looking up at the crenel. Kit stood near her.

She wiggled further through the hole until she felt the opening grasp her around her hips. Her legs still dangled in the crypt. She kicked and twisted, trying to pull herself free, but she was stuck.

She held out her hand, pushing against the outside stone wall with her free one.

Kit grabbed hold of her wrist, as did Rafe. Both pulled.

Mercy shifted and kicked her feet, trying to get free. She suddenly felt hands on her ankles. The guards!

Desperation and fear overcame her. She kicked hard and hit one of them.

The boys pulled, tugging her forward.

The guards tried to yank her back. She could feel a set of hands grasping each leg now. Their strength pulled her back. She looked at Kit with anguish. "Rafe," she called. "Take the boys to safety. Kit, go with him."

He shook his head desperately.

The guards pulled hard on her legs. She slipped back, her hips were free now and she knew it would only be another yank before she was back in the castle. She clung to the outside wall desperately. "Do as I say," she commanded, and then immediately regretted her harsh words. "I love you, Kit."

And then the guards pulled her back into the darkness of the castle.

Richard spit on his manacled wrists. He used the spit as a lubrication, but even that was not helping. His skin was raw and burning from his attempts at freeing his hands. He would have to cut off his thumb to have a hope of slipping the manacles from his wrists.

He saw a light through the iron bars of the door. It was coming toward him. He straightened. He might have a chance of overpowering the guard. He was not giving up.

Through the slotted door, he saw two guards. One held

a very bright torch and Richard had to squint. The other had his sword drawn.

That can't be good, Richard thought. "Evening meal already?"

They unlocked the door and swung it open. "Stand up, heathen."

Richard sat for a long moment, debating his options. In the end, he stood. One guard grabbed his arm and pushed him forward, down the dungeon hallway. He almost tripped but righted himself.

The corridor had only one torch. It was musky and warm. The clangs of the guards' armor echoed through the corridor.

The guard with the sword was right behind Richard, the tip pressed against his spine. It would take little effort to knock it aside and bash the guard in the face, disarming him. The guard with the torch was at the rear.

The guard poked him in the back with the sword, urging him up the stairs. It was time. Richard stiffened, preparing to act.

"That woman was a feisty one, eh?" The guard holding the torch asked.

Richard froze. Woman?

"She didn't kick you in the face."

Tingles of unease danced up Richard's spine. He glanced over his shoulder to see the sword-holding guard had a fat lip.

"The bishop was not pleased with her."

Richard took a hesitant step up the stairs. Was she in the dungeon?

"Get moving," the guard commanded him.

Richard took another step. Should he find her or wait to make sure it was her? He knew. He knew it was Mercy searching for her son. And now the bishop had her. The best way to help her was to be free. He spun, knocking the sword aside and plowed his elbow into the guard's face. As the guard went down, Richard grabbed the sword from his hand.

The guard holding the torch dropped it and reached for his weapon.

Richard smashed the end of the sword into his head. The guard dropped to the ground.

The first guard groaned.

Richard grabbed his hauberk and pulled him close. "Where is the woman?"

The guard gaped, confused.

Richard shook him. "Where is she?"

"The bishop has her. They were waiting for you."

A hard punch across the guard's face with the pommel of the sword knocked him out. Richard searched the guard for the keys to his manacles. But there were none. He didn't have time to search for them. He had to reach Mercy.

Chapter Sixteen

Mercy stood in a small room with a golden table situated on a raised dais. A thick wooden cross was positioned at the front of the altar. Before it, Bishop Devdan knelt, his head bowed in prayer.

A guard stood on either side of her. She looked around, but the room was barren except for the two steps before the wooden cross. She had been waiting for the bishop for what seemed like hours now. But he didn't move, he simply knelt there. The one saving grace for Mercy was that the boys had escaped. They were gone and the bishop couldn't hurt them any longer. She found satisfaction in that.

Finally, he moved. With a sigh, he clutched his golden staff and used it to rise. He looked old. Frail. He turned to her and regarded her with cold eyes. Shrewd eyes. Angry eyes. "You must be proud of yourself."

Mercy lifted her chin.

"You think yourself clever."

"Relieved, now that the children are safe."

"Safe? They were safe here. They were sheltered. Well fed. Taken care of. I took care of them. I loved them."

"*I* love Kit! He is *my* boy. You have no right to take him from me."

The bishop hobbled down the stairs, moving toward her. His fingers clutched the golden staff. "Yes. You were the most vocal about the children."

"People died because of what you did!"

"The children do God's work."

"What work did they do?" Mercy demanded. "What work did a child do that a grown man could not?"

He shook with rage for a moment, his eyes widened in outrage. Then, he took a deep breath, glancing at each of the guards. "It is not for you to say."

"It *is* for me to say! Kit is my son! I am his mother. There is no better place for him to be than at my side!"

"Ahh. Kit. He is a special boy."

Tremors moved across Mercy's shoulders at the inappropriate way he said Kit's name.

"I am delighted I found him. So...innocent. So..." He looked at her. "I can't get enough of his blonde hair. So fair and...lovely."

Disgust filled her and she yanked away from the guard's hold. "He's gone! You'll never get your hands on him now!"

The bishop nodded. "It is a shame that I lost him. But there are so many other boys." The bishop puffed out his lower lip and his eyes glinted. "I will have to be satisfied that you will never see him again."

Realization silenced her. He was right. Kit had escaped. But she had not. Despair filled her. They were still separated. She would never show the bishop that he was victorious or that he had hurt her. She lifted her chin. "But neither will you. I saved him."

Suddenly, a door opened behind them. Mercy turned.

Richard charged in, sword raised before him. He dispatched one guard before he could draw his sword, and whirled on the other.

Richard had come! Joy exploded through her.

Suddenly, the bishop lunged forward, moving with astonishing speed. He grabbed her arm and pulled her back against his chest, placing the golden staff across her throat. He tugged the rod against her throat.

Mercy pushed against the staff so she could breathe as she watched Richard battle the guard.

Swords clanged through the room as metal met metal again and again. Both of Richard's hands held the hilt of the sword because they were still manacled together.

Mercy's hands hooked over the staff, trying to pull it from her throat.

Richard knocked the sword aside and lunged, impaling the guard. He pulled his sword clear and whirled. He froze. He locked eyes with her. "Let her go and we will go," Richard told the bishop.

The bishop growled, holding Mercy tightly. "Put your sword down."

"Or what?" Richard demanded. "Will you kill her? Killing is a sin."

"You should know." The bishop grinned. "Other guards will be here soon. They will have heard the fighting. I can't lose."

Desperation washed over Mercy. She gazed at Richard. They had been so close. No! She had to do something! Mercy's hands tightened over the staff and she shoved it. But the bishop pulled it tighter against her throat making her gape for breath.

"You would kill her in retribution for the sin I committed?" Richard's hands tightened around the hilt of the sword.

"You will not win. Sinners are not victorious," the bishop proclaimed.

A dull clunk. The bishop loosened his hold and Mercy shoved the staff from her neck, ducking out of the bishop's hold. She stumbled forward into Richard's waiting arms and looked back at the bishop.

The bishop was on one knee and Rafe stood behind him with the heavy cross from the altar in his hands.

The bishop turned to Rafe as Richard took a step forward.

Rafe lifted the cross again and smashed it against the bishop's face. Bishop Devdan dropped to the ground.

Richard raced to Rafe and stood before him protectively. He stared at the bishop on the ground, his sword at the ready.

The golden staff rolled from the bishop's fingertips down the stairs and across the stone floor until it came to a stop in the middle of the room.

Mercy ran to Rafe and pulled him against her, holding him tightly. The boy struggled for a moment and then his shoulders slumped. He began to sob quietly, trembling as he stared at the bishop's body.

The cross fell from his hands to land softly on the floor.

Mercy turned Rafe from the grisly sight and murmured soft words to him as she steered him across the room. She glanced back at Richard, horrified and relieved.

"It's alright," he whispered. "We need to get out of here."

Mercy nodded and began toward the door. They would have to go out the front door. Richard would never fit through the small opening in the crypts.

Richard followed them.

Mercy glanced back to see Richard standing over the bishop, glaring at him with a snarl.

"With any luck, they'll say I did this. I'll gladly take the blame," he said.

The bishop's white robe was stained with red. A trickle of blood was beginning to flow down the stairs. "Not all men of the cloth are holy," Richard whispered. "Monsters come in all forms."

"Richard," she called.

He lifted his gaze from the bishop and looked at her.

The twisted repulsion left his face as he stared at her, dissolving into wonder and appreciation. He hurried after them.

Chapter Seventeen

Their escape was tricky. Richard didn't fit through the hole, so they had to walk out the front door. They used the disguise of monks wearing robes, to cover Mercy and Richard. Surprisingly, no one stopped them. They walked out the front door, through the wards, and since the sun had risen and the gates were open, through the front gates.

They retrieved their horses and collected the boys. Then proceeded to Goodmont.

As night set, Mercy sat beneath a tree, gazing at Kit who slept beside her. She was so grateful and relieved that he was unhurt and at her side again. It was all because of Richard. She would never have escaped if it weren't for him. Joy and contentment blossomed inside of her.

Kit was safe. It felt as though a huge weight had been lifted from her shoulders. She reached out and brushed a strand of hair from his forehead. Her stare shifted to the other children stretched out on the hard ground. Some slept alone, arms stretched out, some huddled with other children. They had saved all of them.

She lifted her stare to Richard who sat opposite her. He was staring at the manacles that still bound his wrists, his brow furrowed in contemplation.

A fond, proud grin slid over her face. If it wasn't for him, they would still be prisoners of the bishop. He had rescued all of them, her more than the rest. She had been lost without Kit, afraid and alone. She suddenly realized this was the first time they were not planning an escape or hurrying the children to a safe place. They were safe. Desire to be near him, to touch his strong body, filled her like a deep breath of air.

He turned to her as if she had called him.

Flames erupted inside of her. She wanted to kiss him and stroke him and touch him.

As if reading her thoughts, he stood and held a hand to her. His manacles clinked. One of the children turned.

Mercy rose quickly, before she woke any of the children, and crossed to him. When she took his hand, he led her just a few steps from the children but still within sight of them.

She gazed up at his face, so perfectly chiseled, so tempting. "I never got to thank you."

He brushed a thumb along her cheekbone. "No, you didn't."

She grinned, remembering the time he said that to her. Her response had been the same as his. Tingles danced along her skin, following his fingertips. "You came back for us."

He grinned. "Of course. I'm not really a brute." His gaze softened and longing filled his stare. "Lord, Mercy. When I heard Devdan had you, I thought my world was done. I had no choice but to help you. I had to see you safe."

Mercy slipped her arms around his waist, stepping in until their bodies touched. "I'm glad you did."

Richard lifted his manacled arms and she ducked beneath them.

"We really have to do something about those shackles," she said. "When we get to Goodmont, Frederick will free you."

His gaze swept her face with hunger before he dipped his head to claim her lips.

The heated stroke of his lips sent waves of desire pounding through her. She held him close, giving in to his kiss, exploring his mouth with hers.

He groaned and pulled away. "Lord, Mercy. You drive me wild. I want all of you."

"We'll be alone soon enough," she promised.

"I plan to honor my vow of having you in a heartbeat." He caressed her back, drawing her against his hardness. "But I will wait until the children are safe and we are alone."

A slight sigh escaped her lips. She couldn't wait.

Mercy held Kit tightly as they led their horses down the dirt road. The children ran around the horses with an abundance of energy and excitement. They were close to Goodmont.

Richard took up the rear, guarding all of them. He felt like the Pied Piper, leading the children. Of course, he was not leading them to death but to hope. What a group. How he, an excommunicated knight, had found himself responsible for so many children, he could not fathom.

His gaze found Mercy as she set Kit down. The child scampered away to chase another boy.

She watched her boy for a moment before locking gazes with Richard.

He grinned at her, the heat sizzling between them. She swayed her hips and he knew she felt it also. She continued down the road.

He wondered if she would settle in the town again. He knew he would do anything to make her love him as he did her. He'd come to appreciate not only her beauty, but her mind. She had rescued the boys. Without him. Every time he thought of it, it brought a smile of disbelief to his lips.

Rafe hurried down the road and then raced back. "Do you think my mum will recognize me?" Then he rushed down the lane again.

Mercy smiled.

Rafe was a wonderful boy, and Richard would have been happy to have him as a son. The boy had proven himself to be a fighter. And a survivor. He was sure part of Rafe's attack on the bishop had been hatred for what the bishop had done to him.

As they topped the small hill, Mercy lifted her chin. She was no longer afraid to return to the village. Still, Richard saw the way her eyes hardened and her jaw clenched. This could never be her home.

The sun rose high in the sky as they approached the first field. A woman working in the long stalks of wheat looked up as the group approached.

Rafe froze. The boy had wanted to return home. Mercy insisted he be their first stop. He turned to look at Mercy.

She nodded encouragement.

Rafe walked slowly toward the woman as the group stopped in the road. It had been four years, four long horrible years for Rafe and his mother.

Mercy reached out and Richard took her hand, sensing how nervous she was for Rafe.

The woman came forward to greet them, wiping a strand of dark hair from her forehead. She held a basket on her hip. "Can I help ya?" She squinted in recognition. "Mercy, is that you?"

Rafe paused just feet from her. "Mum?" His voice wavered.

The woman looked him over from head to foot and scowled. She glanced at Mercy and then Rafe again. Slowly, realization dawned on her face and her eyes widened in surprise.

"Rafe?" She took a tentative step forward. "Rafe?" She dropped the basket and ran to him, enfolding him in a tight embrace.

Richard grinned at the sight. Relief filled him. His mother welcomed Rafe. It could have been much worse. Like Thomas's mother who never wanted him and sold him to the bishop. But Rafe's mother welcomed him joyfully.

Richard tugged Mercy on. The rest of the children grew anxious to see their own families.

"Mercy!" Rafe's mother called.

Tingles danced down Richard's spine. Would she condemn Mercy now?

As Mercy hesitated, Rafe's mother came forward and embraced her. "Thank you! May God bless ya ever more. Thank you!"

They continued on into the village.

Frederick the blacksmith removed the manacles without question. He told them Bishop Devdan was dead. Word had travelled quickly. Some mourned him, some rejoiced. He had been murdered, but they didn't know who did it.

Neither Richard or Mercy commented, and the group moved on. The scene was replayed over and over as they returned the children. All of them except for Luke and Thomas. Kit and Luke played behind the horses, running and chasing each other while Thomas drew in the dirt of the road.

Mercy stared at them for a long moment.

Richard moved up to her side. "They will live with us."

"Us?" Mercy asked, shocked.

Richard balked. He ran a hand through his hair. "I just… Where else…?"

"Why would you want to live with me?"

Richard's eyes widened in surprise. "Do you have someone else you want to live with?"

She shook her head. "I just assumed –"

"You are amazing. And stubborn. And dedicated. And so damned lovely." His gaze swept her face, and then a scowl came to his lips. "The question is do you want to live with me?"

She stepped closer to him so that their bodies were just touching. "After what you did?"

He dropped his head in embarrassment. He had committed a crime against the church that would send any woman in her right mind running in the other direction. He couldn't blame her. He had believed he was doing the right thing, the king's order. He would take it back if he could. But he couldn't. "I'm sorry for what I did."

"You shouldn't be! You were magnificent. If it wasn't for you, I would still be the bishop's prisoner."

His eyebrows rose in shock and he finally saw the teasing smile on her shapely lips.

"I know what you did. And you have more than redeemed yourself in my eyes. You saved us. I couldn't ask for anything more."

Richard shrugged. "You could ask for someone with more coin. Or perhaps someone who isn't hated by almost every villager in the realm."

"*Almost* every villager. But not by me." She took his hand into hers. "I've found you rather attractive since the first moment I saw you."

Richard grinned. "You thought I was handsome."

"I thought you were *very* handsome. The most handsome man I've ever seen."

"It must have been the bruises on my face. Or my swollen lip." She brushed a lock of hair from his forehead. "Mercy. I would have you as my wife but think on your decision. I am a wanted man."

"I am a wanted woman."

"Wanted only by me. They know nothing of your part in the bishop's death. You are still innocent."

"I am far from innocent."

"I will take you with me to Knaresborough Castle. We will be safe there. Hugh is a friend." He framed her face in his hands. "I love you, Mercy."

"Are you certain?" she asked hesitantly.

"More than anything in my life. Can you open your heart to a man like me?"

"I already have. I love you with all my heart." She stood on the tips of her toes to press a kiss to his lips.

When she would have ended the kiss, Richard bent and held her close, deepening the kiss. Lord, he loved her. How had he become so lucky? She had shown him what forgiveness was. She had shown him mercy.

The End

ENJOY THIS BOOK? I COULD USE YOUR HELP

Reviews are the most powerful tools I have to get attention for my books. Just a simple sentence or two of why you enjoyed it would help other medieval romance fans find my books. I would really appreciate a moment of your time and an honest review!
Thank you!

THANK YOU

Thank you for reading Mercy and Richard's story. I hope you enjoyed the tale of powerful love overcoming such dark evil. I have many more exciting novels for you to read, so please join me on my adventures into the medieval era!

A Knight With Mercy is Book 2 in the Assassin Knight's series. Pick up **A Knight With Grace**, Book 1 in the Assassin Knight's series.

Stay tuned for Book 3 coming soon! You can stay up to date with all of my releases by joining my newsletter!

Thank you for reading!

Welcome to my world!

Laurel

ABOUT THE AUTHOR

Critically acclaimed and bestselling author Laurel O'Donnell has won numerous awards for her works, including the Holt Medallion for A Knight of Honor, the Happily Ever After contest for Angel's Assassin, and the Indiana's Golden Opportunity contest for Immortal Death. The Angel and the Prince was nominated by the Romance Writers of America for their prestigious Golden Heart award.

When not writing, you can often find her lounging with her five cats or researching ideas online for the next book. She loves to visit the Renaissance Faire, spend time with family and hear from her readers.

She finds precious time every day to escape into the medieval world and bring her characters to life in her writing.

Subscribe to her newsletter so you don't miss out on upcoming new releases and fun contests. http://bit.ly/laurel-odonnell

Thank you for reading!

Made in the USA
Coppell, TX
13 April 2023

15566964R00100